The
Witchball

Frogmella Divine

For
Mum & Dad
with love

Witch ball n. *a hollow sphere of glass hung in windows in 18th century England to ward off evil spirits, witch's spells or ill fortune. According to folk tales, witch balls would entice and capture evil spirits with their bright colours.*

Be careful who and what you play with…

ACKNOWLEDGEMENTS

My heartfelt thanks to
My family for your encouragement and support
William Felstead for technical help and cover design
Sylvia for your wisdom and kindness
Jon and Simon for the inspiring good times

Not forgetting
the power stations
the power trippers
the power zappers
& the power sappers
who crossed my path
& laced my life in silver

1

Alex stared at the photograph through whiskey weary eyes. There was nothing special to set it apart. Their house was full of similar snapshots. Looking around, each one transporting him back to past times just like a paper time machine.

He thought back to that day he had surprised Mia with tickets to New York remembering the joy in her face as they finally stood, side by side, under the Statue of Liberty. It had been the place she had always longed to go and he had proposed on that very spot. Glancing now as he did at the photo of their spring wedding he found himself momentarily back there.

These photos that she had proudly displayed around their new home told the story of their shared life. The happy arrival of Grace followed not too long after by the arrival of Ben. Looking around now he saw how their snappy twosomes had fast become happy family foursomes.

Staring intently at the gold gilt-framed photo he

clung to it tightly, scanning for clues; why had he picked this one with so many to choose from on display? How happy they looked. Mia's blue eyes sparkled. She was wearing a green dress. It was forties style, feminine. Ending just below the knee it showed off just enough leg. He had always liked her legs. She was tall. It had been a long time now since she had stood on those long legs.

Cursing the thought from his mind Alex met Mia's eyes. They seemed different; no longer the blue of their summer holiday seas. He looked closer into this snapshot of his wife's eyes. Eyes he had not looked into since Grace's party. They were definitely green. Knowing Mia's intense hatred for anything fake, contact lenses were out of the question. Maybe it was the colour of the dress bringing out a different shade in those lovely kind eyes; a reflection, perhaps?

Suddenly it dawned on him why he had chosen this picture. It was the last one they had taken together before everything had started to go wrong. He looked into those green eyes again. *Had she been suspicious then?* He was sure she had. She had become clingy and desperate for reassurance. Traits previously alien to Mia. Jealous almost. *Oh Mia why didn't I listen?*

Hanging on the old oak mantelpiece were four homemade stockings neatly graduating in size from large to small. Mia had designed and sewn each one, painstakingly personalizing them with her love. Alex's was the largest and simplest, fashioned in a cosy cream knit. Just looking at it now filled him with fond memories as warm as the Christmas jumper that his mother had herself knitted when he was a boy. Too small and too dear to throw away, Mia had worked her magic on it and the resulting stocking had graced their every Christmas together since. Only Mia would not be here this Christmas.

Her stocking was next in line. Slightly smaller it was velvet red in colour with satin buttons resembling an Edwardian boot complete with decorative laces. With its distinctive wide toilet shaped heel the sharply elongated boot tip upturned and spun back on itself reminding him, in that moment, of a Catherine Wheel. It dangled from a large candy striped bow of green and red.

The children's smaller stockings were next. Grace's pink and full of frills and bows and bells. Ben's a smaller version of his father's, made from the right arm of that very same mothballed jumper.

The room looked different, smaller with the twinkling lights of the Christmas tree now dominating the bay window against the backdrop of the rainy and miserable late afternoon. No sign of the white Christmas Mia and the kids had been wishing for. He wanted Christmas to go away. Sipping the last of the whiskey, the smell always reminded him of festive times evoking ghosts of Christmas past and promises of future fun. In spite of his mother-in-law's pleas he wondered how he would find the strength to get through it 'for the sake of the kids'.

How perfect the tree looked. Each year Mia changed the colour scheme with only the very special collected trinkets taking centre stage, year after year. The same porcelain fairy with the finest white feathers sat at the top of her tree. Keeping her watchful eye on the stripy blue swimsuit wearing Santa, holly emblazoned rubber ring around his mighty waist, his hands clasped together in a mock diving pose, a souvenir from one carefree summer Christmas spent down under in hottest Byron Bay.

The hazy glow of the fairy lights reflected on silver beads and a myriad of shiny glass baubles. Staring now he estimated that there must have been at least seventy of them. They were all sizes, all perfectly spherical, all perfectly shiny and all silver. All perfect.

Needing another drink he headed for the kitchen. The silence of the room was broken by a short glug glug as he poured another drink from the now nearly empty whiskey bottle.

Across the kitchen table lay a brown envelope. Forcing himself, he opened it and took out the photographs of the party which Herb had taken and printed himself. Flicking through them now he stopped at one of Grace, her excited face lit by the light of the candles on her birthday cake. Ben, his top splattered with jelly and ice cream sat next to his sister, himself and Mia stood behind. His father-in-law had caught the magic of the moment; they were all smiling. Mia's mouth was slightly open. She had been singing as the shutter clicked.

Immediately next in the pile was another, almost identical, shot. Only closer inspection would reveal the different faces of the two women in the otherwise familiar three. Comparing the two photos now, Alex noticed that the women's hair colour was almost the same. It suddenly occurred to him that it hadn't always been. Jayne had been a red head before taming down her tresses to a more subtle rusty brown. Mia in turn had added fiery autumnal copper shades to her usually brown hair. Why hadn't he noticed before?

His heart ached with a physical pain. How stupid he had been. Mia had been right all along. Yet he had ridiculed her, called her mad, insane even. It had just seemed too unreal. He hadn't been able to fight it. Jayne's seemingly magnetic presence in their life had just happened. Yes, it had just happened but what exactly? The familiar fog that permeated his memories surrounding that woman was ever present. Like his mind had thrown a cloak over events, he just couldn't catch those elusive memories. All he had were fleeting flashbacks, nothing solid or tangible, just remnants of some other reality.

He took another swig of the numbing alcohol. Who was he trying to kid? He shook his head. He could not fool himself. He was a grown man. A capable, intelligent man. He threw the photo with Jayne across the table in disgust; disgust at himself and his pathetic behaviour.

Now as the dusk fell, he looked around the kitchen. Stumbling across to switch on a light, his attention turned to the large shining ball which hung above the patio door. The reflecting light had brought it to life. Keeping his eyes firmly fixed on the hanging ball he stumbled slowly backwards and took another seat at the table.

He picked up the bottle. Not the whiskey bottle this time. His now swimming mind was still capable enough to tell him that drink was not the answer. There was no answer; this was all too strange for him to understand. The bottle he now held was small. It was made of glass. The old fashioned kind; like an old medicine bottle. He noticed the contents were a much paler colour than the amber brilliance of the whiskey. This was much paler, a diluted whiskey colour; very diluted. He wondered if his urine would be this pale. He doubted it. Especially with the amount of whiskey he had been taking down recently. He would wager a bet that there would be very little difference in the colour.

He stared at the long metal nail that stood in the bottle immersed in Mia's pee. His lovely Mia. Even her pee seemed pure. The bottle was firmly secured with a cork stopper. Remembering back to the time in the garage when she had asked him for the long nails she had been cagey about their use and he had been too busy and too disinterested to pursue it. Then he had forgotten all about it. Until earlier this evening when he had, whilst drawing the curtains, accidentally knocked the little black cat ornament off the window ledge. His searching hand had poked around blindly attempting to retrieve it from behind the headboard, puzzling when instead he had found the little bottle. Mia was not there to ask what it was. A quick web search had thrown up few possibilities. He was not able to protect her. She was trying anything to protect herself now. She had been truly frightened. He hadn't listened. His anger rose again. It had never been far away since all this had happened; an all consuming, destructive, anger.

'Well what good did these do you Mia?' he screamed as he launched the protection bottle through the air in the direction of the witchball.

2

Mia and Alex had fallen in love with their new house immediately. It was a beautiful Victorian house in the country. Perfect. Complete with an established lilac wisteria winding around the front door and creeping around the upstairs windows. In fact, it was everything that Mia had dreamed about. She had attempted to contain her excitement. It was slightly above their budget and without her salary now, she wanted Alex to be sure. So she kept tight-lipped as they promised to let the agent know and headed home.

The countryside here was pretty. Especially that day as the sun shone and the wildlife busied itself all around them. The sweet smell of wild flowers and blossom on the breeze, every now and then rudely interrupted by the acrid smell of horse dung as farmers fertilized their fields.

On impulse Alex pulled into a pub. They still had a couple of hours until Grace needed picking up.

'It's a big step Alex.'

'It's the next step Mia. Are you hungry? I am. What's on the menu?'

Alex ordered, scampi and chips with peas twice, and came back to the garden table with a large glass of red wine for Mia along with one of those table numbers on a wooden spoon.

'Thanks Alex but you drink that. I'll drive back.'

'You ok, what's up? It's everything you've always wanted isn't it?' not needing to be told twice, he took a large slurp of the wine, 'We can do this Mia.'

'Remember it's not 'we' anymore Alex. We need to do our sums. Without my salary things will be tighter.'

'Not necessarily. Without Grace's nursery fees and travel costs,' he paused, 'Ok we'll do the sums and make sure. Business is good Mia. You will be able to spend real time with Grace before she goes to proper school. And if we're lucky we'll have a brother for Grace soon.'

'Maybe sooner than you think,' she had smiled as she told him, 'It's not confirmed yet Alex but I know, it's the same weird feeling as I had with Grace.'

The barman turned up with their food, 'Do you want sauce with that?' he had never before seen people so excited about a lousy plate of scampi.

Alex had been so happy even when she reminded him that his order for a boy may still yet be delayed. All their hard work finally seemed to be falling into place. They had negotiated a deal through the agent and Mia had stayed on at work for a few more months as the maternity leave money would help with the extra expense of the new addition to their family. Then Alex's order was right on the mark with the arrival of Ben. They had all settled in to their new home and new roles well. Grace loved her new brother and having her mummy at home.

Mia loved being home too. There was little she missed of the rat race in London. She felt like she had been granted immunity on the shit side of life. She had said goodbye to office politics, the backstabbing and the little people with huge egos, treating each other like shit, bullying and manipulating their way to the top. She had wanted out for a while. It was becoming more and more difficult to retain her integrity when all around her had long since sold theirs even for just a sniff of the next rung of the corporate ladder. Her jaw had started to ache as she had been almost perpetually gritting her teeth towards the end.

She'd had occasional flashes of 'clarity' whilst around her ex-colleagues. Some lied. She could see it and their two faced, destructive natures. Of course, most didn't know she could see through them. She had come across some, with her blossoming traits, that must have had an inkling, for these were encased in an impenetrable invisible bubble, the force of which she could feel. Some others were transparent to her although she was wise enough not to reveal as much.

If she arrived in the office to a colleague's proclamations that she'd had a great weekend, when Mia had seen a film played out in her head of her row with her boyfriend, she told no one. Nor when she instinctively knew of someone's latest backstabbing action. When they had patted her on the back at her latest event delivery success, they were ignorant to the fact that she could 'see' the glinting invisible dagger that hand had also grasped.

They hadn't all been like that, thank goodness. Carol was an ex-colleague turned friend and one to surely keep hold of. That was Mia's philosophy when she found a good 'un, keep hold of them; they were few and far between.

Having escaped from all that now, life had settled down and she started to do all those things she didn't have time for before. Well maybe not all of them but she enjoyed running up the odd pair of curtains and she certainly cooked a lot more these days.

Her parents were coming over for lunch. She suddenly remembered she should check there was wine in the fridge and some beers for her dad and Alex. It had taken them months to get the place just so. Mia had done as much as she could with her growing belly. Alex had sanded the woodwork and floors in the evenings after work and at weekends whilst she had painted the woodwork. It was hard work but they took it in their stride. There wasn't any spare cash to hire in help so Herb and Pearl did all they could to help too.

After Grace's room was painted in the brightest bubble gum pink, Mia's only other priority was getting the nursery ready for the baby's arrival. They had decided not to find out what she was carrying. At their age there were so few surprises left in life that they looked forward to finding out on the day when he or she finally arrived. So with that in mind, Mia had chosen a fresh, linen white for the walls which could, if she felt like it and had the time, be easily changed later. She was beginning to like the whiteness of the room. Sometimes, when she was alone, she would sit in the room soaking up the stillness of the blank white surroundings. In contrast to the bright reds, purples and greens of the rest of the house, the room felt new and untouched, perfect she thought for a new baby.

She sat there one day in the empty room, on the floor as they had yet to get any furniture, and let her mind wonder. There was a time when all this, the life she had now, one with her own family, had seemed a distant road and one which she had often thought that she would not travel. Her life had unfolded just like everyone's does. She had clutched her bump and wondered what life would hold in store for the little one safe inside.

Soon the house was finished apart from the drawing room which they had left until last as a few of the floorboards were a little tatty and needed replacing. They had earmarked the room for a dining room although they preferred to eat in the informal sunny surroundings of the kitchen.

Alex had gone to collect some reclaimed floorboards and her dad was going to help him lay them that afternoon. She made the most of the snatched half an hour alone to give the place a quick dust.

She had lost touch with so many friends when she moved away. It was always like this. She found it so hard to maintain friendships when there wasn't regular contact. After a little time had passed she had a sort of automatic grieving process for them. It was beyond her control and came unannounced and in the most unlikely ways. Perhaps a song that reminded her of them on the radio. Suddenly she would remember the person in the past tense and that was it. Subconsciously it was done. She found it very hard to then meet up with them. After all, to her they were no longer registered in her present, nor she in theirs it would seem. They were merely somebody she used to know, that had once known her. Too much time had passed, too many things, good and bad had happened. She wasn't that person they had known anymore. Nor, she suspected, were they. What would they talk about? The past? All that had happened since? She couldn't see the point. If their friendship had been that important it would have stood firm, not blown away seemingly unnoticed in the constant winds of life with all its ensuing routines and dramas. She always tried to keep important friendships alive. After fruitless efforts what followed was to her inevitable and happened the world over; she had merely let them go.

And so her world had shrank somewhat but she was happy. The smell of polish filled the air as she sprayed and wiped the duster across the tall black statue. The monotony of house work always made her mind wander. She thought back to living alone; sometimes weeks could pass without the 'need' for dusting. To her it had been one of the perks to just ignore the dust and cultivate the cobwebs and she had herself nicknamed her last little flat Havisham Palace. Dusting always made her think too much; besides there were so many more productive things to do.

She studied the black form. It was one of her favourite things. Alex had bought it for her for her birthday when they had not been together long. She'd had it a long time now. It stood in the front window about a foot and a half tall. It was a woman's form complete with long hair, long legs and rounded curves in all the right places. He had said that it reminded him of her. When she had admired it in the shop window one day, she had thought no more about it, it was expensive. What a lovely surprise it had been when, months later on her birthday, she had unwrapped it.

She heard the front door. All her family arrived at the same time and in an instant the quiet peace was over.

Mia and Pearl got started on cooking dinner just when the two men came into the kitchen for a tea break.

'You only started twenty minutes ago, what's this, a go slow?' said Pearl setting out the tea cups.

'Look what we found under the old floorboards,' Alex put something covered in tissue paper on the table and went across to the sink to wash his hands.

'What is it?' asked Mia looking at the covered round shaped parcel, tied with string; it reminded her of one of those scented bath bombs she bought her mum for Christmas.

'Looks like an old bath bomb,' her mother said exactly what Mia had been thinking.

'Open it Herb.' Alex dried his hands on a 'places to visit in Cornwall' tea towel.

'No thanks I hate those smelly things at the best of times.' Herb ignored his wife's knowing smile. She knew he wasn't averse to them; she had slipped them in the many baths she had run for him. He had told her once he especially liked the fizzy apple type.

Mia reached across and picked it up. The paper was dry and some of it disintegrated in her hands as she tried to undo the string.

Grabbing a pair of kitchen scissors Alex snipped it away, freeing the curled brown paper which cracked and fell like decaying confetti to the ground from

Mia's hand.

'What is it?' said Alex.

'I don't know. Look,' she offered it across so they could get a better look, 'It's not a bath bomb,' she tapped it, 'It looks like wood.'

They all took turns in looking at the wooden object which had been crudely but painstakingly carved. There was no consistency to the pattern just an array of random and unequally sized digs and dents in the dark brown wood.

'Strange one,' was all Herb could offer.

'Perhaps you should just put it back where it came from,' said Mia. 'Somebody obviously put it there for a reason.'

The two men set to work again, stopping only for lunch and they finally hammered the last board in. Alex tidied away his tools putting the hammer back in his tool box. *Shit!* There before him was the carved wooden ball in the new piece of silver paper Mia had found and carefully retied as best she could with the original string. Lifting the tool box drawer he quickly hid it in the shelf beneath. He was damned if they were going to pull up the floor again just to put that back. He looked across at Herb who, watching him, just raised his eyebrows.

3

That night had passed uneventfully. Grace had slept right through the night and, for once, so had Ben. *Bliss* thought Alex as he continued getting dressed for work. He had mastered the art of doing so quietly now as Mia was still sleeping and he didn't want to wake her. He looked at her. She was lying on her back, the quilt covering her body apart from her right shoulder which was exposed. He leaned across to cover it. Seated on the edge of the bed he began to knot his tie. Ben started to cry loudly in the next room.

'Mia. Wake up Mia. Ben's crying, I'm late for work.'

When she didn't respond he gave her a gentle nudge. The baby's cries were getting louder now. Still she didn't move. He leant across getting closer to his wife. He could see that her eyes were open wide. She didn't blink. Staring ahead, she didn't move.

The baby cried. He gave her a gentle shake.

Mia could see Alex. She could hear Ben crying.

Something was wrong. Although she was willing her legs to swing off the bed she couldn't make a move. She must get to her crying child. Only her body wasn't responding. What was this weird feeling of her limbs moving although they were not, in reality, moving at all?

She was watching from above now recognizing the sheer panic in her eyes. She could feel it too although in a sort of strange way the feeling didn't belong to her.

Ben's cries were becoming louder and louder. She watched as Alex shook her. She didn't respond. She couldn't feel his touch, which she could see was getting heavier as the fear rose in him. He was panicking. Ben was screaming now. Suddenly, Mia too, let out a scream.

'What the fuck happened Mia!' Alex was finally able to speak. She was back.

He was late. He couldn't hang around. She must have been dreaming he thought, as she went off to see to the children. Probably just having another one of those lucid dreams she had told him about.

He must remember to ask her about it tonight, he thought as he fired up the car engine. He couldn't miss his scheduled appointment. It was a breakfast meeting with Tina Trough. Known crudely around the office as 'Tina! Tina! The old Prick Teaser!' she expected to be schmoozed by him personally; no one else would do, she insisted. She was a big contract so he indulged her even when she repeatedly crossed and uncrossed her legs in front of him and he was in danger of seeing her breakfast.

He was tired and his mind wandered during the meeting. Until… there it was again, way past its sell by date and laid out on a plate. Years of waxing and plucking had resulted in sporadic baldness. The remaining thin wisps of pubic hair looked like cheap curled up garnish added by a desperate chef in an attempt to spruce up a tired, unappetizing dish.

Agh. The things people do for money. She, he had decided way back, was never going to be one of them. How glad he was that she was not his woman. Averting his eyes he thought of Mia. He had lost her once all those years before. He thanked his lucky stars again that he had finally persuaded her to come back to him. He blinked away the memory and was glad when Tilly the secretary came in with more coffee. He had primed her, or rather bribed her earlier to come and save him. It was well worth the cost of her annual subscription to her favourite trashy magazine.

Mia dropped Grace off at pre-school and picked up her mum on the way. Pearl had shown concern for her daughter the moment she got into the car. She knew instinctively, as mothers do, that something was wrong. Mia had decided not to go into the events of this morning preferring instead to reassure her mother that everything was alright and that she was just feeling a little tired.

Mia enjoyed their shopping trips. It was a good opportunity to talk; just the two of them and it was always helpful to have her mum on hand if Ben decided to start crying mid-shop. She was doing this now, fussing proudly over a gurgling Ben as they chatted between putting food in their trolley.

'You're just worrying too much Mia. You have had a lot on your plate. What with a new baby and a new house.'

'Alex was the one that wanted it. We had enough space. I said I didn't think the timing was right to move. We should have held on.'

'Well you know Alex. He's just like your dad. Stubborn as a mule.'

'That's just it Mum. He was over there to tell the McKenzies we'd decided to hold fire. They'd been so kind we thought it would be best to go over. Deliver the news in person rather than cold from the agent.'

'Well I never. You didn't say they put the screws on. And they seemed like such nice people too.' Spotting the stacked cans of tomato soup, Pearl walked across the aisle.

Mia's eyes locked on a man coming towards her. There wasn't enough room for him and his trolley to pass. She felt icy cold; as cold as the eyes boring into her.

Pearl, noticing her abandoned trolley was causing a hold up, apologized and wheeled it to make enough room for the man to get through. He said nothing, eyes still fixed firmly on Mia.

'Did you want some Mia? I'll grab it for you.' Pearl reached for some more tins.

Instinctively, Mia turned her back as the stranger walked on by. She shuddered. Only he could see that he had ruffled her feathers.

'Cold? Me too Mia,' her mum had noticed Mia's change in stance and, feeling suddenly chilly, pulled her jacket around herself, 'It's freezing in here. I don't know why these places have to be so cold.'

The stranger was still looking.

Mia averted her eyes and, regaining her composure, continued shopping trying to shake off the heavy cloying feeling in the pit of her stomach. She walked on as if nothing had happened.

'Hey remember when you were in Australia and me and your dad sent you tomato soup over for Christmas? Cost nearly fifty quid to post it.'

'I know Mum and it was worth every penny, their version isn't the same. I don't know, maybe it's changed now but apart from family that was one of the only things I missed.'

'It was worth every penny then,' she smiled and gave her daughter a kiss on the cheek, 'Anyway you were saying about the house?'

'Oh yeah, when Alex went there they weren't in so he said that he'd phone them the next day. That's the thing. He woke up next morning full of beans for the place again,' as she talked Mia spotted the tins of baked beans and added them to her trolley, 'He said he'd slept on it and that was that. Wouldn't hear what I thought. Said he knew that I loved the place and to leave the worrying about how we'd pay for it to him.'

The two women continued to the next aisle. Mia picked up a hair dye; redder than her usual. *Sod it*, she had been thinking about it for long enough now. She tossed it in the trolley.

'Well you like it there don't you? It's your dream home. You two have worked hard together. Childhood sweethearts. Eh, remember that pokey little place you two had when you first moved in together.' Pearl laughed.

'I used to save some cheese for the mice. I felt sorry for them. I used to sabotage the traps Alex put down. He couldn't work it out. That caused a terrible row at the suppliers.'

In the next aisle Mia took a bag of wild birdseed.

'Still feeding the wildlife Mia?' Pearl smiled, 'You'll never make the hunt.'

'That reminds me I need to get some cheap dog food for the fox.'

'Um and your dad asked me to pick up some fish food,' not seeing the brand Herb had asked for, 'It's out of stock, can we call in to the pet shop on the way back?'

Shopping finally done and paid for the two women were in the car chatting as they headed for home.

'All marriages go through changes love.' Pearl raised the subject again, 'Try not to worry. He's probably just a bit overwhelmed and tired. Just like you are. How about me and your dad take the kids one Saturday night? You two go out and remember who you are again.'

'How did you do it Mum? You had three of us little ones.' Mia kept her eyes fixed on the road as she spoke.

'And I wouldn't have had it any other way. Like anyone. And like you will too. You just get on with it.'

Mia looked at the long road ahead.

'Don't forget to call in at the pet shop, your dad thinks I can't remember anything as it is.'

Minutes later they were outside the shop. Talk about her mother's memory, hers was bad enough and she would have driven straight past it if she hadn't been reminded.

'I'll wait here with Ben.' Mia switched off the engine.

'Oh come in. You know he likes to see the animals.'

Clicking off her seatbelt, Mia relented. How she hated the smell of a pet shop. She'd had a Saturday job in one when she was still at school; the smell took her back to that time in one inhalation. And the noise. The screeching of the birds.

Ben jumped and then smiled gurgling and giggling. Pearl held him up, his face illuminated by the neon blue of the face level fish tanks as he watched the zigzagging bright colours and swishing of tiny fish tails.

Mia wandered across to the birds. Bright yellow canaries sat on perches alongside blue rinse budgies that intermittently flew back and forth in the tiny confines of their caged cells. She wanted to buy them all. To rescue them from their entrapment and set them free. She remembered saying as much to her mother, one Saturday years before only to be told that 'they know no better, the wild birds would kill them anyway, and they wouldn't know how to survive if they had to fend for themselves'. Mia shuddered at the thought. Keeping an animal locked up like that especially a bird just didn't make any sense to her and she would never understand it.

Alex had been on his way back home. Leaving in a hurry like that this morning he had come out without one of his files. He had nipped home quick to pick it up in time for that afternoon's meeting. It had been a lovely sunny day after the incessant rain of the past week so he decided he would take the longer route back and explore some of the country lanes around his new home.

That was when he had passed a car that was stopped on a verge. As he drove on by he noticed the woman driver and heard the engine rev. He had glanced back in his rear view mirror hearing the engine choking as the wheels span in the mud.

Stopping the car on his drive and opening the front door he had called out for Mia. She hadn't been there and the house was quiet.

He had hoped that she hadn't tidied up and put his file away. No it had been there where he had left it. Grabbing it from the kitchen table he thought about making a sandwich but suddenly felt bad for the woman, wondering if she was still stuck in the mud. Looking at his watch he did a quick calculation. He had time to eat then or he could go check on the woman, see if she needed help.

From the way she had been flooring the car he suspected that she would be well and truly stuck fast now. He should have stopped right then but he thought he may have had to look for the file.

Grabbing a banana from the fruit bowl before jumping back in the car he decided to head towards the lane on his way back to the office. Just as he had suspected, the car was still there. As he drew by the side of it he had noticed that there was no sign of the woman. Good he thought. He could stop by that new sandwich bar guilt-free.

Just then she stood up right from where she had been obscured by the car. Her hair was auburn, almost orange, in colour and she cursed the car kicking at its front wheel.

Sighing he pulled over to park up. 'Need some help?'

'I tried to get off the verge, it's too muddy with all the rain. The wheels just kept spinning. I think I made it worse.'

'Alex,' he introduced himself extending his hand, 'I

don't think I have a tow rope in the car or I could pull you out.'

'Jayne,' she shook his hand, 'You went by earlier. I was cursing you for driving on.'

'Yes,' feeling like an utter shit, 'Something brought me back.'

'I may have some chain in the boot,' she opened up the back of the car and started rooting around.

'Anything?' said Alex peering into the contents which included a lot of clay and modeling materials, 'Looks like you could concrete the verge if nothing else, stop this happening again.'

'I make models, you know sculptures and things,' she explained, 'Nothing, just this bit of an old chain belt but I live just across there.' She pointed to her house opposite.

'I'm a bit pushed for time. I have a meeting, can't be late,' he politely took the chain which was flimsy and broken, 'That's not strong enough maybe I could call back later if you can't fix something else.'

'Oh, ok.'

'I have a tow rope in my garage,' he looked at his watch, 'Sorry I have to dash now. Hope you weren't going anywhere special? I could drop you somewhere, if it's close by?'

'No that's ok Alex, I think it can wait. Your meeting it would seem, won't.'

'Ok,' she had made him feel like a naughty schoolboy, 'Well I'll drive by on my way back and help, if you are still here that is.'

Still holding the broken chain he got back inside, automatically throwing it over the back seat before driving off. He was barely at the end of the lane when his mobile rang. It was the office letting him know that this afternoon's meeting had been cancelled. He asked why and Tilly said they had been on their way but had broken down. Seemed it was a day for car trouble all around. He made the journey back home in a couple of minutes.

Mia was still not in so he grabbed the tow rope. He was back in the lane in less than fifteen minutes but he did not expect that Jayne would still be there.

She was congratulating herself silently that, with the aid of the silken spider gossamer strands and her homemade spell, the car had proved an effective web. She had sat in it, spinning her field of capture, a couple of times before but nothing passing had tweaked her fancy.

He pulled up beside her car noticing she was sitting in the driver's seat with the window wound down.

'I am back,' he called out, 'The meeting was cancelled.' He thought it looked like she was waiting for him, like she had been sure that he would be back.

He secured the tow rope and, with the aid of some off cuts of wood he had also found in the garage, the car was soon out of the mud.

'Doddle.' Alex wound up the tow rope throwing it back in the boot. Grabbing an old rag he wiped his muddy hands before offering it to her to do the same.

'Thank you,' taking it she added, 'If there is anything I can do for you just let me know.'

'Best get home,' he felt slightly uncomfortable. 'My wife and kids will be wondering where I am.'

'Really?' she paused, 'At this time won't your wife be expecting you to be at work?'

Closing the car door he left her question hanging.

'Pop back anytime,' she tapped her blood red

finger nails on his closed window, 'Come take a look at my wares.' Still holding the rag, she watched him drive away. 'I'm sure I will have something she likes.'

Mmm thought Jayne; she had taken a fancy to this dark haired stranger. He was tall and handsome in a sort of quirky, geeky way. She liked the way his hair was slightly too long; the way it wisped into curls at the end. The way that he had shown his practical side with the car.

She felt certain that such a man would have a wife even before he had mentioned her. She knew for certain that he had felt her admiration even before he had mentioned his wife; that was surely the reason that he had mentioned her after all? *Mmm*. Could be a tricky one. She knew from experience that, when she had dangled her bait before, the 'married but fuck it still interested kind' merely forgot about the Mrs back home. The 'what she doesn't know won't hurt her brigade'. There were plenty of those around and she was done with them. What she wanted was one with a conscience, all the better for conquering, they were that little bit harder and somehow that made the victory that much sweeter. She relished the additional power surge that came from winning over their internal conflict. In the meantime she thrived on the buzz.

Yes, she was certain that she would have something amongst her homemade wares that would appeal to his darling wifey. For she set about making it straight away, rummaging and retrieving the curvy hag stone she had previously put aside especially for an opportunity like this.

4

It didn't happen very often; only in books or the movies usually. Halloween and a full moon colliding, thought Jayne, rubbing her hands together. She had much work to do.

Cutting the ribbon with razor sharp scissors she threaded it through the holes in the stone concentrating her thoughts and muttering under her breath. The hag stones (how she hated that term) were plentiful in the wood behind her cottage. She found most of them near to the river, some even in the water itself. That's where she had found this one. Other people sometimes called them fairy stones which was just as bad; two descriptions, both being of equal revulsion to her. All different in their shape and size, they all had one thing in common and that was the hole that had occurred naturally as they were exposed to all the elements. With the constant drip-drip of water, in time the stone had grown a hole and, in more time, this had spread until it reached right through to the other side. These stones held magical powers; wisdom gleaned across the years.

What an interesting shape. She turned over the stone in her hand. Twisted and worn into curves it resembled a distorted silhouette of a woman's form. She had been surprised to find that it also appeared to have two holes.

The ribbon passed easily through the first located below the 'waist' of the stone's shape just before the stone widened into what, to her, looked like over enlarged hips. The other hole, just above the stone's curve which resembled a bust where a neck, in her imagination, should be, was filled with dirt. Taking a wooden toothpick she started to dig away at the collection of dried dirt and was surprised when, after only a few seconds and with little effort, the freed toothpick came poking out through the other end.

She looked again at the two-holed hag stone. Special by this alone, its shape had an added dimension; that's why she had decided she would not let this one go, instead she had put it aside to work on later.

Now as dusk was falling, she gathered up the stones into an old style wicker basket and walked around the house collecting other stones, crystals and rocks she had collected over the years. Taking them into the garden she set about placing them on the ground. The moon would be high in the sky soon. She would leave them to charge up, energized by its powerful rays, overnight. Feeling the first spit of rain on her cheek she smiled. *Perfect*. Nature would cleanse away any stagnation before the magnificent moon beamed down its boosting energies.

Back inside she retrieved the curved hag stone from its place on the oak alcove above the fire. The smooth stone felt cold apart from one small area that had been exposed to the open flames. Turning it over in her palm she considered its shape, deciding on its best orientation. This wasn't difficult as the stone was naturally slightly bulbous at the top, twisting and tapering down in a slimmer shape before blossoming out again into a second, more ample, almost symmetrical curve. A perfect foundation for a charm, the two time-channeled holes were perfectly positioned; one slightly to the left of the top curve, the other in the centre of the lower.

Taking some clay she kneaded it, working it, making it more malleable with the heat of her hands and in the heat of the fire. She started first at the top, pinching and rolling a small sausage shape as she fashioned a neck, squeezing the clay between her thumb and forefinger. The work was delicate but her thoughts, as she worked away, were anything but. Using her fingers in a circular motion now she nipped off the excess clay leaving just enough to form a head which she smoothed and shaped. Next she started to work downwards, taking another piece of the clay she fanned it out, moulding what would become the neck support over the upper curve of the stone. The natural undulation looked like a bosom and she was careful not to overlap the clay too close to the hole through what would be the heart chakra of her model. Happy with the upper half she carefully unpeeled it from the stone and, taking some wire, she used it to support the open end of the clay.

Next she started work on the lower section, taking a larger chunk of clay she worked down from the widest part of the rock making an overlapping skirt that would attach, again avoiding the lower hole; the base chakra of her doll. All the while her head filled with thoughts, not a loving one amongst them. She tapered downwards from the curve forming the lower part of the body. Using a scalpel she fashioned the v where the legs met and traced a groove downwards, deeming the legs useless and there purely for decorative affect. Pinching the end of the clay into a slight curve she finally shaped the tightly closed feet, which pointed outwards and upwards. Prizing the bottom carefully away she shaped more of the wire to ensure that the clay did not warp.

The fire was almost down to its embers now so she added another log, pushing it back and watching as it caught and smoked before it started to flicker and burn orange. She took a handful of some other hag stones and placed them in a circle in the powdery grey embers, just out of reach of the lapping flames. She winced once or twice with the heat, pulling her hand quickly away between adding more small rocks so that she had two little stone circles on either side of the fire. In one she placed the clay 'top' and, in the other, the clay 'bottom'. She added a couple of extra rocks to the back end of the circles just to give added protection from the lapping flames. The flames reflected in her eyes, their heat bringing a corned beef complexion to her cheeks, she uttered her incantation, the fire in that brief moment, sputtering forth a plume of black smoke.

Excited with her work, she almost forgot to put the special two-holed stone outside. Placing it on the grass not far from the others, in the distance she heard the faint whispers of children playing trick or treat.

She rose with the lark the next morning only it sounded more like a crow, a big black noisy screaming crow. Opening the back door she shooed it away and collected up the stones and crystals she had left out the previous night. She counted them as she placed them back in the basket to make sure that they were all present and correct; she held the special hag stone separately in her palm before placing it on the kitchen windowsill.

Putting the range on she started to gather the ingredients together for the biscuits; fresh ginger and hawthorn, flour and butter. She stirred the mix almost on autopilot and dropped it, bit by bit, onto the baking tray which she then shoved into the oven.

Next, taking the special stone with her, she retrieved the clay forms from the now dead fire. She brushed the embers from the two skirted shapes she had made. Finding the tube of silicone glue, she carefully glued the clay legs and then affixed the top of the poppet to the stone, all the while her mind concentrating on those jet black curls.

It dried quickly. She held it out in front of her, twisting it in her hands surveying its shape; she was pleased with her work and had stopped only briefly to take the biscuits out of the oven. The clay had dried into a mottled grey colour not unlike the tones of the natural stone. Not happy with the shade of the loins she set about mixing together some colour wash. Reaching into the open fire she took a great pinch of embers, stirring and muttering under her breath she used her trusted old wooden spoon to mix the now darkening contents of the little cast iron caldron.

She found the rag, the one Alex had offered that she had kept hold of and, carefully dipping in a corner, used it to dab firstly along the cracks before smudging the liquid across the figure then laying it out to dry on an old newspaper.

Using the shovel and brush from the old companion set she swept up a generous scoop of the black-as-black coal dust. Adding it to the remaining liquid it thickened dark and glistening, the only sound the black batter bubbling slightly as she stirred.

Taking the pipette from her old wooden box of tricks, she squeezed the rubber top, filling the glass vial with the dark liquid. She spoke her incantation again in an almost inaudible mutter as she, squeezing the rubber bung, released the liquid into the holes of the stone and watched as the newspaper underneath became soiled and then sodden with the escaping blackness.

5

Mia was in the garden looking through a recipe book the day that Jayne had walked into her life. Ben was beside her asleep in his pram and she was enjoying some peace and quiet when she'd heard a voice call across the back fence.

'Hello. Anyone home?'

Mia had ran across to the back gate to find Jayne standing there holding a basket filled with freshly cut flowers, cookies and what looked like a pot of homemade jam.

'Ssh. Sorry. Hi. He's just off,' she gestured to Ben in his pram, 'My new one is not a very good sleeper. Guess I was spoilt with Grace.'

'Jayne. I live...' she pointed in the general direction, '... down the lane.'

'A poet,' Mia laughed, 'Sorry sleep depravation, temporarily lost my manners,' she continued, extending her hand, 'Mia...I live...here.'

Jayne didn't take it instead gesturing with full hands as Mia pushed open the gate, inviting her into the garden and the two women walked together back to the patio table and pram.

'Come on through to the kitchen. Would you like a cup of coffee?' Mia offered.

Jayne was about to follow through the open patio doors, when she suddenly stopped. The albeit familiar feeling still took her by surprise, stopping her in her tracks. Already inside, Mia hadn't noticed her impromptu guest hadn't followed her in.

Jayne stood fixated. Mia looked across to see her, still standing outside the doors, her glazed eyes staring upwards. *Strange. What was she looking at?*

'Sounds good,' Jayne finally spoke, 'I'll sit out here shall I. Look after the little one,' she took a seat before Mia could object, 'I'll be as quiet as a mouse, you won't even know I am here.'

Nodding Mia went inside. A few minutes later she came back through the doors carrying a tray with coffee and two cups. She set the tray down on the patio table and started to pour the coffee.

'Cookie?' Jayne offered, 'They are ginger and hawthorn. Made by my own fair hand this very morning.'

'Oh no, not for me thanks.'

'Watching your weight?'

Ouch thought Mia. She had worked hard on shifting her baby weight, how dare this stranger come into her house and be so rude.

'No,' Mia finally broke her stunned silence, 'No actually I used to be addicted to the stuff but it just tastes like soap to me now. Did you know ginger is brilliant for pregnancy nausea? Do you have children Jayne?'

'No,' Jayne eager to change the subject picked up

the jar of jam, 'I take it you like bramble jelly?'

'I prefer strawberry myself, that's my favourite.
Alex loves blackberry. And raspberry. He would eat it
'til it came out of his ears. Sorry, I should explain,
Alex is my husband.'

'I know.'

'Of course, sorry. It doesn't take much to work
that one out, hey? Find myself explaining everything
now, since having the kids…'

'No,' Jayne interrupted, 'I mean I know Alex. Well,
I met him. It was a few days back. He was very kind;
my old banger was stuck in the mud. He gave me a
jump start and pulled me out.'

Mia wondered who this flame haired woman was.
Why was she here? What did she want? She was one of
those guarded impenetrable types Mia could not easily
read. *What exactly did she have to hide?*

'Oh, yes of course. I think I remember him
mentioning something now.'

As Mia spoke the words she wondered where they
had come from. Alex had mentioned nothing of his
encounter with this mysterious redhead. She
wondered why. She had so many questions lately.
Probably it was just having too much time on her
hands to think. Alex had not mentioned this
insignificant meeting because, well because, she
rationalized, it was insignificant. Feeling as though
Jayne could see right through her white lie, her cheeks
were becoming red hot at the thought.

'They say that lack of sleep affects the memory
too,' said Jayne with a hollow laugh.

The space between them fell silent again. A cloud
floated in front of the sun causing the light to dim
and the temperature to drop. Mia shuddered hugging

her cardigan.

'Well thank you for calling by Jayne. And for the bits,' she said exaggerating the checking of her watch, 'I really need to be getting ready to collect Grace now,' standing she put the cups back onto the tray. *Thank goodness* she thought as Jayne, taking her prompt, stood up getting ready to leave. Forcing a smile she added, 'The gift really was very thoughtful of you.'

Later Grace was settled at the kitchen table with her felt-tip pens and colouring book, concentrating hard on not going over the edge. Her latest masterpiece was a dog, a colouring book sort of basic poodle. Its right ear was now a slightly darker shade of pink than its left. Mia arranged some fish fingers under the grill.

'Can we get a dog Mummy?'

'No Grace. I told you before. When you get to be a big girl. If you still want a dog, you can get one then,' she walked across to the table with some place mats, 'Now come on Grace. Dinner's almost ready. Put the drawing away now so we can use the table. Quickly, Daddy will be home soon and the fish fingers are nearly ready.'

'Ok Mummy. I love fish fingers. Can I put it next to the one I painted for Daddy?'

Taking the book Mia carefully ripped out the page. Grace got up from the table and walked across to the fridge to display her creation. Using red letters from the magnetic alphabet fridge magnets she proudly displayed the picture saying the letters out loud. Next to the dog picture was a very basic drawing of a car stuck in mud being pulled by another held in place by a magnetic question mark. Grace stared at the magnet as her little fingers traced its shape as she tried hard to remember what the shape meant. Hearing Alex's key in the door Grace turned and rushed to greet him.

'Daddy, Daddy!' her arms outstretched as Alex scooped her up into his arms and kissed her.

'Hello Grace. Have you been a good girl today? What have you been up to?' he put his daughter down on a chair at the kitchen table and took his jacket off. Smelling the dinner cooking he made a face clearly not sharing Grace's enthusiasm for fish fingers.

'Um. Fish fingers…my favourite!' he said sarcastically pulling a face at his daughter, making her giggle.

After dinner Mia performed the usual nightly rituals, bathing Grace and reading her a bedtime story; Goldilocks again, Grace's favourite. Tonight Mia had made it to the point when the bears had returned home to find Goldilocks sleeping in baby bear's bed before Grace had fallen asleep. Now she was all snuggled up and breathing softly. Mia kissed her gently on the head.

She checked on Ben making sure the baby monitor was on. He was also sleeping soundly. She hoped he would sleep through tonight. The tiredness caused by the broken sleep was definitely taking its toll. She felt exhausted, it was all she could do to walk past her open bedroom door and not go in. Catching sight of her bed it looked so inviting. She had changed the sheets today and couldn't wait to get in it. She turned down the sheets in glorious anticipation, sitting down to flick on the bedside lights filling the room with an instant cosy warm glow. Just five minutes she told herself leaning back on the pillow.

Within what seemed like seconds her tired body felt asleep although her brain was clearly awake. It was giving the message to her limbs to get up, five minutes had passed; to no avail. She could see clearly the white sheets that she had freshly laundered. She was half in, half out of them and looked down to catch sight of her leg to see if it was fulfilling the message she was instructing it; to move.

She could feel it moving but as she watched she saw nothing. She must be dreaming. She woke up. She was. *Thank God* the feeling of paralysis was horrible.

Suddenly overcome in a second she was back there. *Asleep?* She couldn't move. Her brain pleaded with her body to move this time. The feeling was scary. She didn't like it. What did it mean? Had she had a stroke? Was she dead?

She felt her head being pushed down onto the white sheets. She could smell the fabric conditioner. *Agh*. She fought back. Nothing. She was bent double now her body contorted and twisted with the invisible force that was restraining her. She tried to move her arm; feeling it swing into the view of her eye line but when she looked she saw no sight of it. She struggled and lashed out with all her might and concentration, silently screaming at her body to wake up.

She felt frightened, terrified; it was futile to fight so, instead accepting her predicament, she stopped struggling.

When she came to, her head was firmly resting on the plumped up pillow and not embedded in the sheets and duvet at all. Her dreams were getting weirder; she was becoming frightened to sleep at all. Sighing in exhaustion she made her way downstairs to the lounge where Alex was sitting on the sofa. She switched on the baby monitor.

'Good day Alex?'

'Bad day.'

The sound of the television, which they were both now half watching, was all that broke the silence between them. Mia picked up a magazine and started to flick through, glancing at the photos of the less than flattering celebrity 'stolen whilst they weren't expecting it' shots. They never seemed to talk anymore; not unless she forced a conversation.

'I think Ben is teething.'

'Teething? Alex's eyes remained firmly glued to the television as he spoke, 'Don't you think it's a bit early for that?'

'Well maybe it's colic. I don't know.'

'Maybe he's just different from Grace. You said yourself she was a really easy baby. You just need to relax a bit. You always say they pick up on stress. How about a glass of wine?'

'Alex you know I can't, it's bad for Ben.'

Alex got up heading for the kitchen. Mia was quietly seething. It must be hormones. Hormones and physical and mental tiredness she reasoned to herself.

'But don't let me stop you,' she spoke quietly, under her breath almost before wondering why. It's not as if he could hear from the kitchen anyway. He hadn't even noticed her new hair colour; she doubted he ever really saw her at all these days.

Alex took a wine glass from the kitchen cupboard and wandered across to the fridge. It was one of those large double fronted types. The kind with a drink dispenser on the front and a little ice-making gadget. He had wanted one for a long time but the kitchens in their previous homes had never been large enough. He smiled with a pathetic sense of achievement at this latest status symbol. A fridge a status symbol? He laughed at the thought. It was just as he pulled at the door handle that he noticed Grace's painting. It was painted with the simplicity of a child's hand but there was no mistaking. It was clearly a small red car being pulled out of mud by a much bigger black one. Just like the scene days before when he had helped Jayne. Only Grace had not been there. He shook off the coincidence.

That night Ben cried on the hour. It had to be the worst night since he was born. The following morning, Mia was in the kitchen making coffee and toast and now he was sleeping soundly in his cot oblivious to it all. She wouldn't wake him. Maybe Alex would drop Grace off at pre-school and then she could grab a few hours of sleep. Through blurry eyes she placed some marmalade and Jayne's homemade jam on the table. Grace was eating a boiled egg, enthusiastically dipping in soldiers.

'Alex! Toast is ready!'

'I am late. God is there nothing you can give that baby to sleep? I can't go on like this. I need some sleep.'

'That baby is your son, remember? Mum and Dad have offered to babysit one night.'

'I know.' Alex chewed on a piece of buttered toast as he spoke.

'How do you know?'

'I asked Pearl. I wanted to take you out for dinner

and needed to fix the date so I could make reservations. We planned it a few weeks ago. I booked The Green Man. Lucky to get a table really.'

'Thank you.' Touched by her husband's thoughtfulness she leaned across the table to kiss him.

'Finished Mummy,' said Grace peering into her empty egg shell, her mouth smudged with yellow yolk.

'Good girl. Don't forget to smash through the bottom so witches can't rest there,' said Mia leaning across to help her smash through the bottom of the shell with a spoon, 'Now go and wash your face for pre-school.'

Alex felt chuffed he had done something right for once.

'I mean it, thank you. I know that I've been a real grouch. I'm just so tired.'

'You and me both.' Picking up the jam, he studied the homemade label.

'Another thank you I think!' the happy tone of Mia's voice a minute ago had disappeared. She grabbed angrily at the jar, just as Alex was opening it and it fell to the table, its sticky dark red contents going everywhere.

Upstairs the baby started crying; the sound was now in stereo, through the open door and over the baby monitor from on top of the fridge. The biscuits and the other offerings were still in the basket which Mia had also shoved out of the way on top of the fridge; along with the other contents was the, as yet unseen, hag stone effigy.

'Look I'll clear this up. You go and check on Ben.' Alex was checking his watch as he made the offer.

'Forget to mention meeting her did you? Seems

like you made more than an impression on her!' Mia stomped from the kitchen to check on Ben.

Taking a cloth from the sink Alex wiped up the spilled jam. Retrieving the lid he was about to screw it back on and put it in the bin. Instead he paused, spotting a little bit of jam left in the bottom of the jar. He looked across unable to resist. Grabbing a spoon from the drawer and scrapping out the residue, he tasted it.

6

Jayne worked at the kitchen table moulding the clay with expert deft fingers. She took another chunk of clay rolling it into a ball in the palm of her hand muttering as she manipulated the soft material with the fingers of her other hand. She liked the feel of this clay. It came cellophane wrapped and ready to use. It was easy to work and designed to be slow baked in the oven. She had rubbed her hands together on discovering it, as her kiln had recently given up the ghost.

She had selected the material in the flesh colour variety for this project. Using a wooden toothpick she added detail. Pushing the piece of wood deep she fashioned a hole in the shaft. The range had been warming for a while now on a low heat taking the chill off the room. She laid her creation on an old baking tray and slipped it into the oven.

Catface meowed for food. She had earned it thought Jayne scraping out the tin into her bowl. The black crow she brought to the back door this morning was just what Jayne had asked for. Its talons were an essential element to the brew she was making. The clay baking would take an hour and a half. She would have a bath whilst it was firing.

Turning on the taps she thought again about seeing if she could get the kiln, that she'd had built into the stone wall on the ivy entangled patio, fixed. She had missed it initially but, like everything else, she had got by and now she had found an alternative. Like most things in life really she thought. You can get by without almost anything when you have to. Given time and a little patience something always came along to fill the void. She undressed. That's where she had gone wrong many times before. Patience had never been her strong point. The little she had, stretched to breaking point, had finally stretched too far and she had snapped. Her cover blown she had to keep her head down for a bit.

She noticed her bare feet. She hated them and the way they looked. So uneven, misshapen and twisted. She kept them covered up as much as she could. Reaching over for her hard skin contraption she started filing away at the rough dead skin on the soles of her ugly feet. She thought back to when she had met Colin. He had been an easy target. Married for twelve years he was well overdue his seven year itch. He had married early and his mind was ripe with wondering thoughts of greener grass. Their secret and hotly denied liaisons had slowly chipped away at his wife Louise and had driven her mad. Colin had called it a day when he'd gone back home late one night to find his wife rocking slowly back and fourth in a corner by the washing machine, the kids screaming and crying that mummy had 'lost her marbles'. Livid

at the time that all her hard work had gone to waste
she had learned a lesson. Alex was a long game and
she had perfected her play. Colin was just a warm up.
As was Darren. And Matthew. Single men had just
never held the same attraction for her. Anyway, she
wanted more than the man. She wanted the life and
the children.

There was a time when she had used her special
ways for good but that time had long since past. As
an adult the hard knocks of life had caused her to
question and ultimately reject the good girl upbringing
her parents had instilled in her long, long ago. Playing
fair and being kind just hadn't worked out for her.
More and more people had played on her kindness
and energy, finally using her up. She was spent. Flat as
a pancake. Emotionally dead she had joined the
legions of humans that go through life barely
functioning, life having chewed them up and spat
them out. Time marched on. She became trapped and
twisted, old and baron.

Thinking back now to how her anger had
bubbled; the memory was clear as yesterday...

She deserved this. How dare this not work out!
The feelings came bounding back. Seething she had
picked up the wooden apple from the bowl. She had
been fashioning fruit from wood. Bananas, apples,
oranges. She found the repetitive work concentrated
her mind and thoughts. It seemed strange to her the
meaningless dust attracters that people filled their
homes with. Still the shop had taken them, as many as
she could knock out. Some in their natural wooden
state others hand painted to look like almost real
wooden pieces of fruit; providing an ever present
display on hand for people too busy to buy the real

thing.

She looked at the apple its rich brown hues covered and disguised by layers of glossy green and rosy red blush. This apple would never perish or wither with age and decay. For it was not real.

In anger she had thrown it at the wall, watching as the delicately attached fragile stalk splintered away. Throwing the wooden piece against the wall, again and again, she simmered and seethed. With every throw she spat out her destructive thoughts and when she had eventually came to the smudged colours, now smashed off the wooden object, were a splattered mess of evidence on her kitchen exposed brick wall.

The object had no longer resembled an apple. Stripped back to its bare wood it was battered and tired looking. She remembered she had studied it finding a small area where the ruby red paint clung fast. Finding some sand paper she had rubbed it away destroying the last remnants, until all traces were gone.

Then, taking out her knife she continued to dig and stab at it allowing her remaining anger to spill over like a blowing volcano. In her random jabs the knife had slipped slicing through the palm of her hand and she had screamed out in pain.

Looking at her hand she recalled how she had watched as the blood collected in the crease of her palm, tracing slowly along the length before filling in her lifeline. She remembered dropping the wooden object in shock but not before the porous wood had soaked some up.

It was all long gone now; as was Colin. He had moved away, a new family had already moved in.

He had called time on her before. She was

stubborn, had her own mind and she was not going to take his rejection lightly. Not that she took it seriously at all. He was weak and wishy-washy; a walk over. So she had ignored him and taken matters into her own hands. She would see the day when she would have the house. If he went then so be it. He had become tedious. He bored her anyway. So full of promises and hot air.

She had taken what he said with a pinch of salt and any initial attraction had long since evaporated. Only she refused to be taken for a fool. She could have just walked away relatively unscathed but that was too easy. She had invested a lot in his bullshit. It suited her too. Did he really believe that she couldn't see through this pitiful little man? His sense of arrogance had astounded her. No she had decided she would teach him a lesson. Teach him once and for all that he was really not that special.

So on that, his latest attempt to call time on their relationship, she had just sat and waited. Usually during these times she would sculpt or create something. She had known that it was only a matter of time before he would call. When he did she had nothing much to show for the time that had passed since. Only the wooden used to be apple that had lain over those long nights on the cold stone floor beside her.

Still lost in her memories now she remembered clearly how the telephone had woken her. There he was on the other end again making his demands. Would she go over he had a spare evening, Louise had taken the kids to her mother's. He was lonely. What else had she to do anyway? He needed to see her. He had something important to say. Putting the phone down she'd picked up the gauged wood. Yes she would go to him. She would take it with her. She was not giving up now she had invested too much of herself already.

So she had walked up the path to Harley Sound, scoffing at the name as always, in the darkness. He had been waiting at the door.

'Quick before anyone sees you.'

She was touched by his attitude; even more pathetic than usual it betrayed his cowardice and contempt of her. She had felt used.

'I can't see you anymore.'

'You brought me here to tell me that?'

'Well I rather thought I owed you that at least,' his voice trailed off as he'd tried to read the emotion in her eyes. Sadness? She was sure to be upset. Disappointed that things hadn't worked out especially after all his false promises. He suddenly felt like a shit. But no, her eyes were far from sad. There was no emotion registered; well none that he could see. Perhaps it had been he that was the fool? For thinking that she had in fact thought of it as more than some passing dalliance? 'I want to help you,' he finally spoke.

'Help me?'

She followed him through to the back room and watched as he rolled up one end of the rug. Lifting up a small section of floorboard he took out a little metal safety deposit box. Then he had offered her a bundle of notes secured in a roll with a red elastic band.

'For your...' he trailed off unable to think of a suitable word.

'Trouble?' she had suggested.

He'd pushed the money into her hand as she

looked on with cold blank eyes.

'I should go.'

'I was hoping that we could, you know say goodbye properly.'

'You paying me for more trouble?'

'This is not easy. Louise has flipped her lid. You knew the score. Please let's be grown up about this. I can't deal with two mad women.'

'You're right Colin. You are under so much stress. It can't be easy for you,' her livid mind was ticking over fast as she spoke, 'Perhaps we need a drink?'

'Yes. Yes that's a good idea Jayne. Thanks for being so understanding.'

In her mind's eye she could still see him, looking back at her, as clearly as if he were standing before her now.

'Drink?'

'Yes. Of course. I think Louise has a bottle of red in the kitchen. I'll just get it.' He had paused to look at the money box still on the table. He considered putting it back. No he had insulted her enough already without the thought that she would be deceitful enough to clear it out during his short absence to the kitchen.

She clocked him looking at the box, her eyes daring him to have the audacity to put it back before leaving the room. It worked. He didn't dare. Instead he had gone on his hurried search of the kitchen cupboards, finally finding a solitary bottle of wine which had somehow escaped Louise's recent drowning of herself in every available drop of alcohol.

Jayne had acted fast. Taking the wooden ball, already secured in some aged paper tied with string, from her pocket she had rolled it in the fashion of a small bowling ball, listening as it made its way along the eves of the floor.

She was standing in the same place when he came back in with the open bottle of wine and two glasses. She had watched as he could no longer help himself. He lifted the lid of the metal box. There on top was the bundle of notes that he had given her earlier still secured with the distinctive red rubber band.

'How dare you!' releasing her venom she had left the house.

So since then she had adopted a new motto; if you can't beat them join them.

The bath was ready now and her feet finished. The powder contained in the unit of the dead skin grater would come in useful she thought putting it to one side. Slipping into the warm salt water she let her mind drift again.

She had thought about moving away but she was too old to start again. Besides she was part of the house; her very spirit was in the bricks and her magic in the mortar.

When alone she had always spent most of her time reading, being creative as little as she had to be to get by, whilst she practiced and perfected her art. Learning to survive on little money she had painted and made models in clay. The less time she had spent with others the better and soon she had fallen into the life of a virtual recluse. She had even found a gift shop nearby that would stock her creations for a nominal percentage. It had all fallen into place perfectly. She hadn't even had to meet people in order to sell her goods then.

That was when she had met Colin; she had been offered a lead for a private painting, in the conservatory of a customer's house. Remembering now she was unsure whether to accept it at the time but Colin had been in the shop on one of her few rare visits to the place to drop off some items she had made. His enthusiasm for her work had been flattering and in a moment of weakness she had agreed to consider his offer. How stupid she had been to fall for such a ruse.

Looking back that was when her problem had started again. People always brought problems to her life. In another moment of weakness and an even rarer moment of loneliness she had succumbed to his advances. They had seen each other a couple of times a week. He came baring all the usual promises of the married man.

Doing all the running, he caused catastrophe in her life. He made her doubt her own judgment not to mention that of his own poor wife's. Lies all around had culminated in the sticky web that had been spun trapping him and the ensuing struggle leaving him too exhausted to deal with his now subsequently demented wife. Instead he chose to stay and 'do the right thing' by helping her find the marbles, after all, it was his fault she had lost them. They had moved from Harley Sound promptly thereafter never to be seen again.

Mentally visualizing a set of window wipers now, on the projection screen that was her eyes, and switching them on she allowed the images to be erased.

She was unsure if the marbles game would work with Mia. She was smart. Definitely a challenge. Still she was working to the same, albeit tweaked, strategy. She suspected that rocking in the corner was not Mia's style. She was a fighter. She had fire in her belly. That much was evident from their first meeting. Using those qualities would be Mia's most likely move. So she anticipated that she would fight fire with fire. Mia would be putty in her hands, as sure as the clay in the oven was. She would keep chipping and bring out the worst in Mia.

Getting dressed she went down to the kitchen. Opening the oven, she set the clay phallic effigy aside to cool.

7

Mia was in the kitchen unpacking shopping again. She put the crisps and snacks in one cupboard, the chocolates and treats in the special chocolate box which also had its own cupboard. She filled the wild birdseed container from the new bag enjoying the whizzing noise of the colourful seed. She loved the wildlife in the garden. She stacked the dog food tins in another cupboard. Occasionally she would leave some out for the wild fox and badgers. Usually on the colder nights only. She knew that she was interfering with nature and their hunting if she did it too often but she justified this with her thinking that even they needed a break sometime. She just about found room in the wild pantry; there had to be at least nine tins of dog food there.

How had she ever found time for a job as well as all this? The thought had been playing on her mind recently. So had the changes not going to work had made to her life. Adult conversation was thin on the ground these days. Still she was looking forward to going out with Alex tonight. They were finally taking up her mother's offer to babysit.

Looking down she noticed a stain on her blouse. She sniffed it. Baby sick had replaced Chanel as her staple perfume these days. She would get dressed up tonight. She started looking through the remaining two bags.

'Shit!' exhausted she put her hands to her head just as Alex came in the kitchen.

'What? Mia, what's up?'

'I forgot the popcorn…it's nothing, it's just bloody popcorn. I don't know what's up with me,' close to tears as Alex walked across to comfort her.

'Mia you are fine. You are just tired. It'll be just us tonight, we can talk.'

'I promised Grace she could have popcorn. She's got the film and everything planned with Mum and Dad.'

'There's still time. I'll go along to the shop and pick some up.' He left, closing the door just as the telephone rang.

'Hello, oh hi Mum,' Mia answered 'I forgot the popcorn so Alex's just gone to the shop to get…' she stopped talking and listened, 'Oh Mum why didn't you say? No of course not, do you need Alex to get you something? No it's not worth the kids picking that up. No. Well, have you eaten anything bad? Must be a tummy bug, Grace's teacher was off with it yesterday. Ok you go and let me know if you need anything.'

Sighing, she hung up. Redialling Alex's number it went straight to answerphone.

'Alex you need to cancel the restaurant, Mum and Dad are laid up with a bug. See if you can still get the popcorn, Grace will be disappointed enough already. I'm going to jump in the bath while Ben's asleep. Shall we get take out?'

Hanging up the phone she checked on Ben who was still sleeping soundly in his cot. Then she poked her head around Grace's bedroom door. She was playing with some toys on the floor telling them about the film and popcorn.

In the bathroom Mia put the plug in the bath and poured in some of her favourite bubble bath. Back in the bedroom she looked at the special dresses and underwear she had laid out ready on the bed earlier. Disappointed she undressed, put on her bathrobe and went back into the bathroom.

Wiping the steam off the mirror she studied her face. Tracing her fingers across the make up free skin, she smiled and studied the fine lines around her blue eyes.

In an instant she was in another bathroom, in the familiar surroundings of her parents' house. The eyes looking back at her now were unlined, the skin a mix of oily sheen and pimples. A strong feeling of sadness enveloped her, as tears pricked her eyes. She jumped at the knock at the door.

'Mia? Mia are you in there, what are you doing?'

She slowly opened the door to her mother; she too looked younger, much younger.

'Mia it will be ok. You're only thirteen years old. Your skin will settle down. It looks far worse in your imagination,' handing her daughter a bottle of witch hazel, 'As you get older you'll realize just how unforgiving some mirrors are Mia.'

Her mother's face was alongside hers now. The two women gazed at their reflections. The same vivid blue eyes. Only Mia's were filled with tears.

'Look at my wrinkles, they won't be passing with time my girl, they just get worse with worry. Look at yourself Mia. You are pretty. Like an angel. My angel. Now smile and stop giving me wrinkles.' Pearl kissed her daughter and was gone.

Mia stood alone returning her gaze to the mirror. She scrutinized her pimples and her frizzy hair, studying closely every detail. Studying her ears she pulled at them convinced that they stuck out. Noticing something on her right ear lobe she moved in closer to the mirror to inspect it. Close up it seemed to be a hair. She tried to brush it off with her hand.

'Agh!' horrified to find it was attached she pulled at the thick white hair. Wincing she plucked it out of her downy earlobe holding it now between her fingers. Close up it looked like the beginnings of a white feather with a small but distinct quill at its root.

'Mummy.' Grace's sudden appearance in the bathroom snapped Mia back to the present.

'Yes darling?' the mirror was completely steamed up as she wiped away at it with the back of her hand. She saw nothing unusual just her forty something face reflecting back.

Alex parked up outside the corner shop. Switching off the car engine he picked up his voicemail from Mia.

'Bollocks!' getting out the car he wandered into the shop.

Fred the shopkeeper was at the till, ringing in a customer's basket contents. The shop was busy, it was

Saturday after all.

'How do Alex, long time no see, how you settling in?' Fred called across without stopping.

Alex smiled. It made him feel good to be recognized. It was a sign of sort of fitting in and the first step in belonging again.

'Yeah Fred we love it thanks, bit of an emergency though. Where's your popcorn?'

'Popcorn. Sorry mate, seem to have had a run on that. Must be the recession, all those stay at home flick nights,' he had finished serving and came around the counter now, 'Checked out back before, won't be in 'til Monday. Trip into town I'm afraid.'

'No worries Fred,' Alex checked his watch, 'wonder how the traffic will be at this time?'

'Hold on for me Alex. Maybe I can come to your rescue?' Jayne had appeared behind him.

Fred met Alex's eyes as he started to ring up Jayne's basket.

'See you Fred, thanks anyway.' Fred nodded without looking up or stopping. Stepping outside the shop, Alex lit a cigarette and bought a poppy from a passing seller shoving the plastic red flower in the pocket of his jacket. A minute or so passed before Jayne came out of the shop.

'I bought the last two bags of popcorn yesterday. You are very welcome to them.'

'Oh that's ok Jayne. I'll hang on twenty minutes or so for the traffic to die down and I'll shoot into town.'

'Nonsense! Pointless, you won't get home for an hour. Mia will be expecting you and getting ready.'

'Getting ready?' Alex was puzzled.

'For your romantic night out,' Jayne explained.

'Good God! Welcome to village life!'

'No secrets here Alex. Everyone knows everyone's business.' She loaded her things in to the basket on the front of her old style push bike.

'I know it doesn't happen very often but it's hardly news.'

'It is around here.' Jayne smiled.

'Well newsflash!' Alex gestured holding both hands up, 'We have to cancel. No babysitter.' He walked towards his car, 'But thanks for the popcorn offer.'

'It's at the house, I'll meet you there in a couple of minutes.' Jayne cycled off not waiting for a response.

He scratched his head. Putting out his cigarette he got back in the car. Taking a right turn down the road directly opposite Fred's, he continued along the little country lane. He passed her red car opposite her little cottage which was set back from the road, private and mostly covered in wild bushes. Turning the engine off, he waited. He was surprised to see that she was already there, at the front gate.

'Well are you coming in?' she called out to him turning to go inside, leaving the door open.

Alex got out of the car and followed. Walking up the garden path, overgrown and green, he felt intoxicated by the many smells and scents in the air. It was herby and sweet, taking him straight back to his student days.

He walked through the front door. He had to step down as he walked under the heavy oak beamed ceiling and through to the kitchen at the back. The house was small and quaint. In the kitchen stood an old untreated wooden table in the middle of the room. Looking around he scanned the shelves of jars all containing different herbs and potions. He jumped as a black cat appeared at his feet. It suddenly occurred to him that he was standing in a cliché.

'Don't mind Catface. She's just impatient for her dinner.'

She half opened a cupboard taking out two bags of popcorn. Not wanting Alex to see that the cupboard was full of it she shut the door just as he stood up again, having bent down to stroke the cat.

'There you are, that'll keep little Grace happy. Now I wonder how can we make her daddy happy?' she was looking deep into Alex's eyes now.

He looked down in embarrassment. Even he couldn't miss this blatant come on. He had to get out.

'Thank you Jayne, really you've done enough, saving me that trip into town,' he opened his wallet to pay her for the popcorn, 'How's the car running? Alright?' desperately trying to find some change and change the subject.

'I know. I am free tonight,' she was looking directly at him again.

He looked back at her and a loaded moment of silence passed before she continued.

'I could babysit…oh you didn't think I was suggesting you took me to dinner!' she giggled suggestively knowing full well that was exactly what she was inferring.

Alex couldn't hide his embarrassment now; he couldn't wait to get out of there.

'Thanks again,' he said tossing some small change on the table and starting for the door.

Reaching into his pocket to retrieve his car keys he flinched. Taking out the poppy he noticed the attached pin. It has just stabbed him close to the corner of his nail, drawing blood the same colour as the flower.

Jayne noticed and taking the poppy and pin from him started fixing it to his lapel.

'It's kind of you to offer, but, well…don't think we are ungrateful but well you know. Mia will only leave the kids with certain people. People that know them. You understand.'

'Well yes. That's me. Just the other day Mia left me with Ben. Did she not tell you?'

'No.' Alex's finger was still bleeding as he looked for a tissue in his pocket, 'No she didn't.'

'Well she must trust me to do that don't you think?'

'Really that is a very kind offer. Maybe next time.'

'Why don't you check with her if it settles your mind? I shan't be offended Alex. It seems such a shame to disappoint her especially as you were lucky enough to get reservations. Come back in and let me get you a plaster for that.'

Again she didn't wait for a response as she went back inside, certain that he would follow.

'Really it's nothing,' he was all ready to go out and wearing his new shirt. Not wanting to get blood on it he licked his finger trying to stop the bleeding.

Looking up again he noticed that she had gone back in. He looked at the car and then at her open door. Not wanting to be rude he went back in the house. She passed him some kitchen paper.

'So are you going to call Mia?' as she spoke she pushed a plate of chocolates across the table.

Accepted one politely and popping it into his mouth a few seconds passed. 'Well I guess I could just

run it by her,' he threw the bloodied paper towel in
the wicker waste paper bin. He was lost in the taste of
the chocolate. It tasted sweet. Perfumed. Without
words Jayne's eyes gestured an offer for him to take
another, which he did since he wasn't going to dinner
now what did it matter.

'Or you could just surprise her. You know
women. We love it when a man takes charge and
makes things all right.'

Mesmerized Alex was silent, still slowly
savouring the chocolate.

'That's a date then Alex, I shall be with you at
seven sharp.'

Saying nothing he just nodded as he left,
forgetting the popcorn which was still on the table.

Jayne smiled as she closed the door behind him.
Back in the kitchen she took the bloodied paper towel
from the bin and put it in a glass jar quickly screwing
on the lid.

Back at the house Mia was still getting ready.
Alex was giving his opinions on everything from
dresses to shoes to lipstick to earrings. He had
forgotten what it had been like getting ready to go
out. He liked watching her get ready, well at least to a
point. It was so rare these days that the familiar
boredom he used to feel waiting for her, seemed to
have temporarily vanished.

She was trying to remember if things used to be
this difficult. Her indecisiveness had seemed to be a
by-product of pregnancy. Or maybe it was just a mini
confidence crisis. You sort of forget about going out
when you haven't been out for so long. It was easier

staying in and she was momentarily glad that this evening's plans had fallen through. She had still wanted to look nice for Alex though and was enjoying deciding what to wear reminiscing on how things used to be. Her spirits were good. She was breaking her no alcohol ban, just for tonight. She felt relaxed. It was like old times. Sensing as much he started to explain about meeting Jayne on the popcorn run, how she had offered to watch the kids and how he had accepted.

'You did what!' Mia's voice had taken on a high pitch quality that threatened to shatter her wine glass.

'She offered. She said you left Ben with her. I was trying to fix tonight. Make everything ok Mia. I knew you were disappointed.'

'Call her,' Mia spoke calmly now in her normal tone refusing to allow that manipulative woman to ruin her night, 'Tell her thanks. But no thanks,' looking at him she added in a louder voice, 'Alex!'

'Mia you are being stupid. She's well known in the village. She was in Fred's…'

'Call her now,' she interrupted, 'Or I will bloody well do it myself. I don't like that woman. She's a fucking predator, it's written all over her. I don't want her anywhere near my family.'

'What's got into you Mia!' now it was his turn to interrupt, 'You never had a filthy mouth. I won't have us made a show of in the village. Now, I've had enough of this bullshit,' his voice calmer now, 'Get your coat. We are going out. Meet me downstairs', he laughed attempting to lighten the mood, 'Double quick or the bogey woman may gobble me up.'

Mia didn't laugh, 'Did you get the popcorn?'

'Shit!' he suddenly remembered not picking it up

from Jayne's kitchen table. It was right next to the chocolates. Those delicious, delicate homemade chocolates.

'What? Are you kidding that's what you went out for!'

'Fred was all out. I was going to go into town but the traffic was bad.'

'Well you were gone for long enough, what happened, where were you?'

The doorbell rang.

8

'I'll get the door,' he didn't answer her question using the doorbell as an excuse, 'Don't be long.'

A quick squirt of perfume, she slipped on her shoes and grabbing her bag from on the bed was not far behind him. The doorbell rang again just as he opened the door to Jayne.

Mia didn't bother with pleasantries, 'Really Jayne there was no need.'

'Nonsense Mia,' interrupted Jayne, 'I'm very happy to return the favour, your husband more than helped me out.'

She seemed tonight to have some sort of south western accent which Mia had not picked up on before. Mia locked eyes with Alex. Just then Grace came bounding in. She was carrying a dolly.

'Hello Grace now what are we going to do tonight? I know we have lots of lovely popcorn.'

Mia threw Alex another look, 'No we don't,' kneeling down to Grace, 'Daddy couldn't get the popcorn, the shop was all sold out.'

Grace looked disappointed until Jayne patted the basket weave bag she was carrying. 'No need to look so sad Grace, look what I have for you here,' she pulled the bag open slightly, encouraging the little girl to peek inside.

Spotting the popcorn her little face broke into a huge smile. Mia was confused at the coincidence and looked to Alex once more. He looked down searching in his pocket for his car keys.

Jayne smiled noticing Grace's doll, 'And what's her name sweetie?'

'She's called Marmie. My daddy got her for me cos she looks like my mummy.'

Mia picked her daughter up protectively. Grace held the dolly up to her mummy's face. The doll had the same long spirally chestnut red curls and a bright red cherry bow mouth.

'See she's pretty like my mummy. My daddy bought her for me.'

Jayne was studying Mia, making her uncomfortable.

'She does look like your mummy,' responded Jayne after a long pause, 'She's a poppet.'

Grace took hold of Jayne's hand, 'Can we have popcorn now please?'

Bending down Mia buttoned up Grace's pink cardigan and kissed her, 'Now you be a good girl. Remember straight to bed after the film and no juice before bedtime,' she noticed her daughter was still holding Jayne's hand, 'Is the car open Alex?' She deliberately turned without a goodbye to Jayne who was wondering off up the hall with her daughter.

'Don't worry, I'll look after her like she is my own.' Jayne headed for the lounge as she spoke without turning around.

Clearly miffed Mia said nothing back instead addressing Alex, 'I assume she has your mobile number already?' heading for the car she didn't wait for an answer.

He scribbled down his mobile number on the pad beside the phone on the hall table.

They travelled in silence to the restaurant. Once inside they were seated near the window. Alex was grateful for the privacy the corner table gave them. Hopefully they could talk tonight and Mia would relax.

'I'm glad you decided to come tonight.'

'It was hardly a decision. Let's order so we can get home.'

'Well we are here now, let's try and have a nice time.' He took the wine menu from the waiter who had been discreetly waiting in the wings to come over.

Back at the house the movie was playing. Jayne heard the baby crying on the monitor. Grace was engrossed in the tv and eating from a clenched little fist filled with popcorn.

'You wait here Grace. I am just going to check on your brother and I'll get more popcorn.' Taking the huge popcorn bowl with her to the kitchen she flicked on the light and opened the fridge, taking out a baby bottle of milk. She paused noticing the child's drawing of the red car stuck in mud. Flicking the kettle on she unscrewed the teat and, taking a small sachet from her pocket, sprinkled the powder into the bottle. It was her own little mix of herbs to calm the little ones. She sprinkled the remainder over the

popcorn. Pouring the boiling water into a jug she left
the bottle to warm in the hot water whilst she went to
get Ben.

Taking Ben and the now warmed bottle she went
back to the living room. Grace took another little
handful of the popcorn as Ben drank his milk.

'I like this popcorn.'

'Good girl Grace, that's Jayne's special popcorn.
Looks like your little brother is enjoying Jayne's
special milk too.'

The baby was already dropping off to sleep.

'Can I have some special juice please?'

'Mummy said you can't drink the juice before
bed, remember?'

'But I want it!' sulked Grace who was getting
tired and grizzly.

Jayne was getting agitated and her tone turned
nasty. 'Do you want your teeth to fall out!' she
snarled, a slow smile forming across her lips to reveal
rotten black stumps.

Grace was shaking and crying. Jayne laughed
maniacally.

'What's wrong with you child? Now come on, if
you really want the juice…'

'I don't want the juice,' she cried between scared
sobs, 'I want my mummy.'

'Now then what's all this about Grace?' She
comforted the child and smiled to reveal a normal set
of pearly white teeth again, 'What is it, do you want
me to tell your mummy that you have been a naughty
girl?'

Feeling sad Grace shook her head, 'I don't want
my teeth to go black and fall out. I brush my teeth
just like my mummy says.'

The film was still playing and a dog bounded onto the screen and barked catching Grace's attention. Distracted she smiled at the television.

'Do you like doggies Grace?' The little girl nodded. 'Would you like a doggie Grace?'

'Yes. But Mummy says I can't have one 'til I'm big.'

'What about if Jayne gets you a doggie?'

Grace thought.

'Would you like that Gracie?'

With eyes wide, she nodded 'But Mummy won't let me. She says I have to wait 'til I'm a big girl.'

'We won't tell Mummy. It'll be our secret.'

'That's naughty.'

'Do you want a dog or not!' Jayne's voice took on its nasty tone again.

Grace flinched. She sat quietly watching the film credits roll, wanting her mummy home to read her Goldilocks and tuck her in. Looking across at the door, which was slightly ajar, she watched as it slowly opened. *Maybe Mummy and Daddy had come back.* Instead in walked a dog; it stalked slowly as it crossed the room to the sofa and sat before Jayne. Grace's wide eyes were glued to the grey wolf now seated at Jayne's feet.

Her reaction to the black teeth alone could have been mistaken by Jayne. But here there could be no doubt. The child could see her conjured apparition of the wolf, of that there could be no mistake.

Back at the restaurant Alex and Mia were eating their main course. He knew that the moment he agreed to let Jayne babysit the evening was doomed.

Mia chewed her lamb wishing that they had just stayed home with a takeaway. She looked at her watch. She would be reading Grace a story by now. Even another round of Goldilocks didn't seem so much of a chore now. She had deliberately hidden the book under the bed. That was Grace's favourite story. And hers. Grace's and hers; no one else was going to read that to her.

Reaching across Alex grabbed her hand thinking that they should skip dessert. Maybe get some ice cream on the way home. He traced his fingers over her delicate wrists when he noticed the bruising. Saying nothing he took her other hand discreetly turning it over to take a sneaky look at the other wrist. Each one had three small brown bruises evenly spaced like the lasting impression of too tight finger grips. He said nothing, maybe she would mention it later. Instead, about to suggest the ice cream to her, he noticed her glazed far away look.

'Something is wrong Alex. We need to go home.'

'Mia. Look why can't you just relax. You really have wound yourself up too much over all this. It's silly.'

'Silly. They are my kids Alex.'

'Yes and they are my kids too. Lets finish this and I'll get the bill.' Ignoring him she was ready to get up and go.

Everyone in the restaurant was looking over now in their direction, disturbed by their raised voices. Alex took his mobile phone from his pocket. Noticing the waiter on his way over he got up.

'Excuse me,' he preempted the waiter's request, 'I need to step outside to make a call. And would you bring the bill please?'

Outside in the chilly dark, he lit up another cigarette, already the last in the pack and dialled home.

Grace was asleep on the sofa, cradling her dolly, the grey wolf lying on the floor next to her. Jayne got up to answer the ringing telephone, carefully peeling the dolly away from the sleeping child and taking it with her. Grace stirred slightly but didn't wake up. In the hall, Jayne picked up the phone.

'Hello. Alex? Yes things couldn't be better here. The little poppets are asleep,' she paused to listen, 'She should stop worrying and be enjoying that lovely food. Stressing will only give her indigestion. Well yes, I see, see you soon then.'

Hanging up the phone, she noticed Alex's jacket that he had been wearing earlier, complete with the poppy and pin that had stabbed his finger. Taking the pin from the lapel she plunged it several times into the dolly's stomach, slowly.

Stubbing out his cigarette he made his way back inside. There he found Mia looking pale faced and clutching her stomach in obvious pain. The waiter was with her, helping her drink from a glass of water.

'Mia! Mia what's wrong?'

'Your wife is feeling a little unwell, sir.' The addition of 'sir' did nothing to detract from the waiter's distinct air of condescension.

'You don't say!' The superior waiter, who looked a little shocked at the response, remained professionally unperturbed.

'Alex I need you to take me home.'

'Yes of course.'

The waiter continued indignantly 'Please allow me to get your coats,' his eyes looking so far down his large, pursed nostrils as if he had located the source of a very bad smell.

Mia perked up on the short ride home. Ignoring that creepy feeling that had developed and festered in the pit of her stomach was not an option. She had been fully prepared to walk out on her husband if, this time, he had chosen again to dismiss her feelings as whimsical.

In reality he wasn't giving it a second thought, preoccupied instead that he really needed to stop for some fags. Now, as they pulled up at their house, Mia's bad feeling lifted slightly. Then, as she spotted Jayne peering out from behind the purple silk lounge curtains, an instinctual anger bubbled to the surface.

Inside the house, Jayne gave a command to the dog. Walking towards the lounge door she watched as it disappeared. Scooping up the remaining popcorn she chucked it in the kitchen bin, putting the empty bowl in the sink, then headed back to the hall. Stopping at the telephone table she picked up the poppy and pinned it back on to the lapel of Alex's jacket. Back in the lounge she put the dolly beside Grace who was still asleep on the sofa, just as Alex turned the key in the front door. Saying nothing Mia walked in to the lounge. She bent down to kiss her sleeping daughter.

'I told Alex. She's been a little poppet,' explained Jayne, 'You look a little tired Mia. Are you in pain?'

Slightly taken aback by the seemingly spot on observation Mia looked at Jayne but said nothing in response. 'I'm off to check on Ben, Alex.'

'Just indigestion. Mia will be fine.' Alex was feeling more than a little uncomfortable by his wife's uncharacteristic rudeness.

'I am going to bed. So if you don't mind Jayne.'

'I'll call you a cab Jayne,' offered Alex.

'Oh, that may be a problem Alex.' He looked a little confused. 'Just a little misunderstanding with Carey's Cars. They told me I am no longer welcome.'

'Well there must be more than one cab firm!' Mia was not in the least bit surprised that others also had a problem with their impromptu babysitter.

'No Mia. Not at this hour. Welcome to village life!'

'Take her home Alex.'

'But I can't leave you like this.'

'Well it doesn't look like we have much choice now does it. I feel better. I will be fine.'

'Well if you are sure.' Jayne smirked.

As Mia scooped Grace up from her sofa slumber, her dolly fell to the floor.

Great thought Alex, *I can get some fags.*

9

Mia signed the letter to Perry with love. She missed him. She searched in her purse for a stamp. She didn't have any. *Shit!* she thought, resigned to a trip to the small village post office. Stuck in a quaint time warp, this post office had only one window and one teller, probably the post mistress herself. Mia knew this from her one and only prior visit.

On this second visit she found herself in a line, with two women customers before her. The same teller was there again this time serving the first woman who was sending a package to America.

'USA?' confirmed the teller, 'Put it on the scales please.'

Great thought Mia watching the woman put the package on the scales. Checking her watch, she had half an hour before she needed to pick up Grace from pre-school and Ben from her Mum's.

Trying to be patient, her eyes started to wander around the cards and other items on display. Jiffy envelopes, Day-Glo pink and lime green highlighters, white chalk and rubber bands. Her mind started to wander. The southern drawl of the 'American package' woman's voice started to fade now. Rainbow colour paper clips. Pencil erasers, the kind with one white and one grey end. Bulldog clips. Mia felt her heckles prickle. Without turning around she was aware that somebody else had joined the queue behind her.

'That's all today,' the 'American package' woman settled her bill with a debit card, 'Thank you.'

Why is she shouting? No one else seemed to notice thought Mia. She shifted feeling uncomfortable, turning her head now to see the guy who had joined the queue behind her. She instinctively stepped forward a bit. There was not much room.

The teller called forward the next customer. Mia took the opportunity to move forward again slightly, conscious of the '*Please respect the privacy of others - stand back*' sign. Positioning her body side on to the man behind her, she noticed that he was wearing a baseball cap. He kept his head bowed but she could still smell the alcohol on his breath. The fumes were swiftly stirred up with stale sweat, the sweet biscuit smell of old frying fat and a smattering of dirty hamster cages. Mia swallowed hard trying not to gag. She could almost see the smudged frowsy smelling atmosphere around him. Her instinct to face down wind of the man was overtaken only by the even stronger instinct not to turn her back on him.

He began to mutter under his putrid smelling breath, as he shiftily moved back and forth on his feet, whilst all the time keeping his face firmly concealed.

'How much longer is this gonna take?' he demanded under his stinking breath, becoming increasingly agitated.

Mia stayed standing side on. Another customer, another woman, joined the queue behind him. The man lowered his head pulling down the peak of his cap. He didn't want his face to be seen that much was obvious. The next customer before Mia was sending several packets, to several places. All the while this rude smelly biscuit man was becoming ever more impatient at the delay.

The teller finished and as the customer left in walked a security guard wearing a protective helmet and carrying a safe box. Raising his visa, he greeted the teller and Mia stepped aside.

'Are you in a hurry?' she asked the man in the cap, looking directly at him.

'Why is she so slow, I've been in post offices with three tellers and seventy customers and got to the window quicker.' He didn't meet Mia's eyes.

The security guard looked across at them and listened.

'Would you like to go before me?' Her direct question forced him to make eye contact with her.

His face, still partially concealed by the cap, looked smudged and out of focus. It appeared to be melting before Mia's eyes; as the features moved and mutated, they were manifesting into another face. Only the beady black eyes remained the same, as in the next few seconds she saw the ever changing faces of this tortured old soul. Her being was gripped with an overwhelming feeling of deprivation. He was going to rob the place. He was desperate. She fought to break her gaze. Staring and blinking so hard had caused her eyes to cry albeit without the usual accompanying emotions.

What just happened? She looked across to the

security guard seeking reassurance. Looking back at her, she knew he could see it too. They both looked across to see the back of the peak capped foiled thief as he bolted from the shop.

'Next!' called out the oblivious teller.

Affixing the stamp Mia posted the letter. The sooner she could get away for a bit and clear her mind the better.

10

Driving home from work Alex stopped at the final junction. Mia had been in an arsey mood when they spoke earlier. Maybe she had that postnatal depression; he would suggest she saw a doctor. On impulse, instead of indicating right into the short lane to their home, he spun the wheel to the left. The illuminated sign of The Feathered Nest beckoned. A recce of their new local was long overdue. Just a swift half, a little 'me time' as Mia called it before he went home to face the music.

Pushing open the pub door, Alex had to bend his head slightly as he walked through. Inside the atmosphere was warm and cosy from the open fire crackling away in all its glory. It was quite busy and as he walked to the bar, he noticed Fred from the shop with a group, none of whom he recognized. They exchanged polite nods.

'Half a bitter please.' Alex raised his voice slightly over the din. Taking his drink he made for a private seat by the widow. *Bloody smoking ban.*

'Looks like you wanna be on your own?' said Fred who, having momentarily abandoned his game of dominoes, was standing beside him now looking even more rotund without his shop apron. Alex was mid-sip so nodded at the vacant seat opposite and the shopkeeper sat down.

'Look Alex. I've been hoping to get you on your own. It's just that there's been some gossip around the village.'

'You didn't strike me as the gossiping kind, Fred.'

'No. I ain't. It's just there are a few things I think you should know. Forewarned is forearmed as they say.'

'Now I'm intrigued. Drink?'

'I'll just grab mine.'

'What's this about Fred?' asked Alex, watching as Fred got up, collected his drink and then made his way back.

He sat back down before taking a hearty swig. 'It's about Jayne.'

Alex studied the froth now clinging to Fred's wiry beard as he waited for him to elaborate.

'Not taking my name in vain are you Fred?' said Jayne half grinning.

The background chatter of the pub fell silent. Alex wondered where she had sprung from. She sure had good timing. Fred stood up giving Alex a knowing sideways glance. Tipping his hat, he headed back to his table of friends. Draining his glass Alex was ready to leave.

'Why you off so soon Alex?'

'I don't know why I came in even. Mia was expecting me home she'll be getting worried.'

'That's a shame Alex. I was expecting you...I mean expecting we could have a drink, get to know each other a little better.'

Aware of all eyes on him, Alex was heading for the door.

'Another time then, Alex? You are always in such a rush.' She spoke the words just as the door closed behind him.

Pulling up at the house, Alex took a few more minutes in the car. This was becoming a problem. He could no longer ignore the realization. It was dawning and tonight he had truly dreaded the thought of going home. Maybe he had been wrong to push for the house move. And then another baby on top of that. Mia was always tired now. Her spontaneity and her laughter seemed extinguished. He was clueless how to make things right. All attempts at trying seemed impossible. And he hated failing. He never failed.

She was in the lounge dozing on the sofa. The room was in darkness, with only the dim light of the tv, the volume turned down to a whisper. She stirred.

'What time is it?'

'It's just gone eight, Mia.' Alex sat next to his wife and leaned across to switch on the side lamp.

'I thought you were coming home,' she squinted her eyes to the bright light, 'Have you been drinking?' she added, catching the smell of his breath.

'Just a quick half Mia. I wanted to check out our new local.'

'I thought we were going to do that together.'

'I just fancied it, ok. Thought I would do something spur of the moment. Not have to plan everything like a bloody military operation.'

'Well thanks Alex. And thanks for letting me know. I expected you home so I left your dinner in the oven. Shepherd's pie. I know you like your cheesy topping crispy. It's still in there. I expect it will be especially crunchy now. I'm off to bed.'

Her words were full of sarcasm but neither of them could be bothered to argue anymore. His stomach rumbled at the smell of his dinner still hanging in the air. Heading for the kitchen he opened the oven, dodging the escaping captured heat. It didn't smell burnt which was a good sign. She had left the oven on the lowest heat, also a good sign. She still loved him enough to make his favourite and she didn't hate him enough to sabotage it. *Even when I do act like a jerk.*

He spooned a generous scoop of the meat and mash into a bowl scraping off the blackened cheese and frazzled slices of burnt tomato. Disappointed he sulked to himself, *that's the best bit.* And it was his fault. He couldn't blame Mia or anyone else. He ate as much of this cardboard imitation posing as his favourite dinner as he could stomach. Too much he knew would sit like a brick in his stomach and keep him awake so he gave up, scraping the reminder into the bin.

Later in the darkness of their bedroom, Mia opened her eyes fixated on a glowing light in the far corner of the room. She saw the shadowy outline of a plump figure dressed in bright shades of purple. She screwed her eyes tightly shut. *Make sure you are awake.*

The sound of her heavy breathing and heart beating were amplified in the stillness of the room. *Open your eyes, you were dreaming.* She slowly opened her eyes, gasping in terror when she saw that the apparition was still there. She panicked with the realization that the drumming heartbeat she could hear was her own.

'Alex!' she screamed.

'What the fuck!' he awoke, startled, lying facing the direction of the intruder, 'What the hell are you doing in here?!' he screamed as he leaned across to flick on the bedside light.

Looking back across again he saw there was nothing there. Mia was shaking and crying beside him.

'You saw her…it…Mia what the fuck was that?' he comforted his wife as she nodded between cries. 'Mia! Go check on the kids,' his voice was sterner now, fraught with urgency, 'Mia! Get up. Check the kids. They may still be in the house. And call the police!'

They both jumped out of bed. Alex scrambled into some trousers, flicking on all the lights as he searched the house. Mia looked in on the baby who was still sleeping. Grace was also sleeping soundly blissfully unaware of the drama. Mia scooped her out of the bed. She stirred slightly but stayed asleep. Heading back for the nursery, Mia sat in the comfy chair next to the cot, gently placing a blanket across her daughter. Alex, finding nothing downstairs, headed back in to the nursery.

'Did you call the police?' he was peering into the cot, 'Thank God the kids are ok. I've had a good look around. Mia are you listening to me?'

She was staring ahead and said nothing in response.

'Mia I said I've looked all over the house. There's nobody here. Did you dial 999?'

'What for?'

'What for!' he screamed.

'Get real Alex. Do you really think the police can help with this one?'

'You saw it? Mia? You saw it too, right?'

'Sure I did. We can't both have the same dream, right?'

'What did you see? Mia! This is important, what did you see?'

'I don't know...' she stroked Grace's head ' I don't know...was it a nightmare?' Grace started to cry. 'It's ok Gracie, Mummy's here,' she comforted rocking her daughter, 'It was just a nightmare, sweetheart.'

It had been past four thirty when they all settled. Mia had stayed wide-eyed watching her children sleep until the sun had come up. Now, getting ready for work, Alex wanted to let her sleep. Picking up his shoes and making his way over to the bed quietly he sat down on the edge, knotting his tie. Ben started to cry. *Too late*. It dawned on him how he must have become too used to Mia's in-built radar; it always woke her the instant a baby started to cry. It certainly seemed to be malfunctioning of late. He definitely didn't seem to have one himself before. Somehow previously he must have been oblivious when in the land of nod. He knew that from the now broken sleep she herself seemed to have no trouble sleeping through.

He looked at his watch. He didn't have time this morning. Not that he had time for this any morning really. He taxed his fuzzy mind by trying to recall what he had on first thing. *Something I can cancel or reschedule?* He remembered he had switched this meeting twice already. These cancellations had been no fault of his but it would still look bad if it happened a third time.

'Mia. Wake up Mia. Ben is crying,' he gave her a gentle dig, 'I'm late for work'. Ben's cries were getting louder. *Boy that kid has a good set of lungs.* Alex leaned across getting closer to his wife. Mia's eyes were open wide. She didn't blink. Staring ahead, she didn't move. The baby was crying. He shook his wife. Mia was frozen still.

Inside she was screaming a silent scream. *Ben is crying, I must go to Ben.* She was trying to move. Nothing was happening. The instructions she was giving to her limbs were not getting through. *What was happening?* She could feel her legs moving but her open eyes saw that they did not physically move. Ben cried louder and louder. She felt hypnotized. Trapped. Alex was shaking her, frantically now. She stared ahead, her rigid body still not responding.

Her eyes were fixed in terror, her mouth making a silent scream. Alex's shakes were getting more forceful as the baby's cries were becoming deafening.

'AGH!' Mia finally exhaled with a loud piercing scream.

'What's happening?! Mia! What's happening?!'

Instructions finally getting though, she ran to her baby, pulling herself together. Grabbing him from his cot, she comforted him, rocking him gently. She felt the coldness of a tear running down her cheek like a trickle of ice and shuddered.

Alex had left for work. They didn't talk about what had happened; this time or last time. It was a familiar story these days though this morning she had been grateful. Unsure of what was happening Mia had started to doubt her own sanity and felt sure that he must be too. She needed to talk things over with someone that would listen and get her own mind straight first. Family life, leaving work and the house move had led to her losing touch with so many of her friends. These days there was still the odd text and email contact but this was hardly the stuff to discuss online with someone she hadn't seen in years. Flicking through the mental address book in her head she had got through to Carol first attempt this morning and luckily she was free to pop over later that afternoon. Or maybe she had cancelled her other plans picking up some sort of urgency instantly in Mia's voice, as only real friends can.

At the same time Mia had booked a last minute appointment with the doctor. She hated going to the surgery. Here in the waiting room she, along with about seven other patients, sat waiting in near silence. Apart from Jonny who was playing up in the children's play area. His mother had told him at least thirty six times now 'Don't do that Jonny!', 'That's naughty Jonny!' and every other variation you could think of chastising the child, with no success.

She wondered why people insisted on bringing their badly trained kids with them; the place was full of germs and disease wasn't it, not to mention ill people that could do without a petulant child. Children should be seen and not heard was the motto that she had been raised by. Although she didn't entirely stand by it as an adult, this was one situation when she actually did.

Please shut your child up. She so wanted to say it out loud. Instead she gave the woman a pitying look exactly like the ones she got in the supermarket when Ben threw the occasional paddy. *Poor woman; maybe she doesn't have friends or family to rely on and had no choice but to bring little Jonny here today.*

The buzzer sounded and Mia Winterflood was lit up in big red letters. She headed to Room C as instructed. She knocked on the door as you do, even though having summoned you, the doctor was clearly expecting your imminent arrival.

'And how can I help you today?' said the doctor just like a supermarket assistant's badge.

'I am having trouble sleeping.'

'Dropping off or waking up again?'

Mia thought for a millisecond about explaining the strange sensations and the visions; surely a fast track open invitation to loony bin central.

'Both.' She settled on the response and came out not two minutes later with a prescription for sleeping pills. Easy as that. She went next door to the adjoining chemists and collected them.

Back at home she spooned cake mixture onto the baking tray. Grace was 'helping' and they were both wearing aprons covered in flour, especially Grace's, its tiny heart pattern now plastered with an explosion of cookie batter.

'Go and wash your hands now Grace,' Mia untied the little apron putting it straight into the washing machine, 'There's a good girl.' Grace ran off excitedly for the bathroom.

'You need a session with Neil,' said Carol 'He'll sort you out.'

'Why is he a psychiatrist now?' replied Mia only

half joking as she opened the hot oven to put in the cookies and set the timer.

'You are not mad. You have something. You know you do. You just need to develop it now.'

'What if I don't want to?'

'You don't have a choice Mia. You wonder what it is all about, looks like you may be about to be shown. Ignore it if you want but you won't shake it. It always comes back.'

Mia nodded in agreement knowing, in all the madness, at least that to be true.

'Promise me that you will call him. Even if you just get some tips on how to handle things if they get too bad. There are ways you know Mia.'

'I know. Garlic. Crosses. Sleeping pills.'

'This is no joke Mia. Things are getting serious. I can feel it. You have been on my mind a lot. I just don't know how far I can go to help you.'

'Don't you think I know that Carol? Just listening to me without judging me is enough.'

'I will always do that. I'm just not sure that is enough now.'

'Carol I am scared. Something big is happening. I am being primed for it. I can feel it coming, I just don't know what it is.'

'Show no fear. Protect yourself. They can't touch you. Show weakness they'll feed on it and feed on you. Look we can see him together if you like. You can ask Perry along too.'

'Don't know how that would go down. They don't exactly have the same beliefs.'

'No but they both care about you. There will be some common ground and where there's not they'll just meet in the middle. For your sake.'

'I've written to Perry he's only just moved to Cornwall.'

'Good excuse to get down there then. You can't have seen his new place yet. Kill two birds with one stone. Your mum will watch the kids won't she?'

'Well I know a whole family visit won't be his type of thing. Anyway, Alex can't get away at the moment.'

'What does Alex say about all this weird stuff?'

'We haven't spoken about it. It scares me so God knows what he thinks about it all.'

'Don't you think that you should?'

'Yes. The time just hasn't been right. There always seems to be something else to sort out and he's been working a lot too. I think he is throwing himself into work so he doesn't have to deal with this.'

'Um. Sounds familiar.'

'Anyway I can't make sense of it all myself and it's happening to me.'

'Don't forget it's happening to him too.'

'He'll think I am going mad.'

'Do you really think so? You said yourself he saw it too. That's not madness Mia. He has seen something with his own eyes.'

'I'll talk to Mum and Dad, see if they are ok to have the kids to stay. It bothers me that they are getting caught up in all this. I don't know if I can protect them.'

'It'll do you good to get away for a few days on your own. Get your head around it all. And the kids would love it with their nanny and granddad too. I would offer but I have that conference in Paris.'

'I'm thirsty Mummy.' Grace came bounding back

into the kitchen.

'Hold on Grace,' a cloud of hissing steam escaped as Mia took the cookies out of the hot oven, 'I'll get you some juice.'

'I don't want juice!' screamed Grace, her over reaction causing Mia to jump burning her hand badly as she instinctively caught the falling hot baking tray.

Mia couldn't sleep. Alex was sound asleep, snoring beside her. She tossed and turned for another ten minutes and then popped one of the sleeping pills out of the blister pack and swallowed it. The burn on her hand was throbbing.

She lay there watching the red minutes flick by on the digital clock. Twenty minutes had passed and she was still awake. *Surely they must work soon.*

Flicking on the bedside light she had been trying to get into her book; The Wizard of Oz. She had first read it at school. Having dressed Grace as Dorothy for a party a few months ago she had found the box set a few days later in a charity shop. Funny she had forgotten that Dorothy's red spangly shoes had originally been silver. Now in desperation to help bring on sleep she tried again to read it. She was looking forward to reading it to Grace one day but first she wanted to read it herself once more. She remembered there were parts in it that had scared her half to death as a little girl. Dorothy had just left the munchkins and the good witch and set off on her journey along the yellow brick road. She loved the way a good book could transport you, the words sparking the imagination and projecting you in to the experience making it, for that time, your reality.

'So you think that you can take on the bad witch and win?'

As she read the words in her head her internal voice told her a story, soothing her in much the same way as she did Grace through their nightly story telling ritual.

'I said, do you really think that you can take on the bad witch and win?'

She scanned the words on the page. Had she lost her place? She tried again to locate the words, scanning the page. Must be the sleeping tablets finally taking effect and making her lose her concentration. Had she lost her page? She turned over to the next and then back to the previous; try as she might, she just couldn't find the sentence.

'Give up now you don't know what you are messing with.'

This time the words were no longer in her head nor was the voice hers. The whispered threat came from the foot of the bed. She strained her ears and eyes. In the semi darkness she saw the smudgy outline of something. The intangible mass swirled and whirled finally forming a solid blackness, a shadow back lit by the landing light. She watched it rise in the air and float through the open bedroom door, cackling malevolently.

She was still looking in that direction, transfixed, as the smaller shadow entered the room. *Ben?* He had started to crawl only recently how had he got out of his cot all by himself? The small shadow took a seat at the bottom of the bed. *A munchkin perhaps?* Silly of her to read a tale that played with her imagination on top of a sleeping tablet.

She was dreaming. She dug her nails into her

palms, avoiding the stinging burn, watching the skin imprint slowly fade as the skin sprang back to normal. She blew on her palm feeling the warm breeze of her breath. Finally she looked across to Alex. He was still sleeping next to her. Assured now that she was wide awake she looked again towards the bottom of the bed, petrified. The small being scorned her.

'Are you afraid?' Its voice was small too.

'Of what?' she spoke back to it using her internal voice too, not out loud.

The little elemental didn't answer. She felt it staring back at her in the darkness. A wave of fear washed over her again.

'I knew it. You ARE scared.' The response was again non verbal and the telepathic voice took on a chilling tone, 'Frightened of going mad Mia?' It was reading her thoughts that was exactly what she was terrified of. 'You are always crossing the planes and now you have taken hypnotics. If you are scared now you don't know what you are letting yourself in for. We'll be waiting for you Mia. See you there...see you there...turn back...turn back...' The contradictory warning of the little voice was getting weaker.

The apparition blurred and pulsated into a black orb changing colour into silver then back again and again as it bounced slowly up and down out of the room to the high pitched strains of the yellow brick road...'follow, follow, follow...' as it and the singing finally faded away to nothing.

11

Mia was asleep. The dream came suddenly. She could see her legs stretched outwards before her as she lay sleeping. They rose, closed tightly at the ankles in a keep fit pose she would, in her waking hours, have been proud of. Yet she knew that she did not possess this level of fitness. There was no effort involved as she felt her legs levitate before her rising slowing with the lightness of a feather. The feeling of elation that she could do this passed quickly as she started to counter the rise, with all her might, to bring them down in line to meet the rest of her reposing body.

She couldn't do it. The attempted downward movement was at once counteracted by the invisible force. Yet she could rationalize that her physical body was not actually moving; this part of her being that usually inhabited her gravity anchored legs, was floating up high above her. The familiar feeling enveloped her and she fought to control the internal panic which, now activated, was multiplying in her brain.

The soles of her feet were now raised upwards facing the ceiling. The suction motion started with a whoosh as she felt her energy being sucked through them by some mighty vacuum. She instinctively fought the feeling, panic overwhelming her again.

Her sleeping mind changed gear; fighting this was pointless. Her instinctive animal response switched from fight to flight as she made the conscious decision not to fight the overwhelming feelings she, in her defeat, accepted them. Then, immediately and with all the intensity and speed of a balloon being popped with a pin, the magnetic pulling ceased.

Panic over, sudden feelings of anger surfaced and she raged at the invisible force, 'Tell me what you want from me! Tell me what you want me to do!' Her screaming pleas were loud bringing her back to reality. For a second she was sure her outburst must have woken Alex but, as she looked across for reassurance, she saw that he was still sleeping beside her.

12

Perry was excited that Mia wanted to visit especially when she had revealed that she was to come alone. He loved kids. Especially when they were other people's and went home.

Mia's parents thankfully didn't hold this opinion and were more than happy to have the kids for an extended sleepover. She had been more than a little tearful as she dropped them off. Phoning again, on the way to the station, only to be assured by her mum that Grace had not cried for her and neither had Ben. Both were watching cartoons with Grandad and had been dipping egg soldiers.

At the station Alex opened the boot, 'I'll walk you to the platform.' He took out her suitcase.

'No Alex. It's ok I can manage,' she had deliberately packed light, squeezing all she needed into the mini size case on wheels, 'You'll get a ticket if you stop here. Now promise me you will keep in touch with Mum. Make sure she is doing ok with the kids.'

'Do you really need to ask that Mia?'

'No. No of course I don't. Look you are more

than capable. I know that. You are a good father.' She leaned across to kiss him.

'It's only a couple of days Mia. I'll be around there every day don't you worry. Now you make sure you say hello to Perry for me. Tell him I said to make sure he looks after my wife.'

'I will be in safe hands don't you worry, if anyone can help me with this Perry can.' Mia instantly regretted the second half of her sentence picking up the slightly hurt look in Alex's eyes.

'Look you have a rest.'

'You do believe me Alex?'

'I don't know what is going on here Mia but we need to sort this out.' As he went to take her hand she pulled away. He was hurt again until he remembered that she had burnt it. Seeing her fragility clearly now, as he took her other hand, he was glad that he hadn't suggested she see a shrink.

'Alex?' She pressed him further not satisfied with his evasive answer.

'Well of course something is going on. I just don't understand it,' he said looking down, 'I can't understand it.'

'I know. I know. Light those white candles every night. And send me your love Alex. I love you.'

'I love you too. Say hello to The Bucket of Blood for me.' They hugged goodbyes and he watched her walk into the hustle and bustle of the lunchtime commuters.

Catching glimpses of the fleeting faces as she passed them, she was hit by a wave of emotions. Worry, sadness, longing, stress, happiness, haste; each face she met with had a strong electrical emotion attached to it. Some of the faces blurred and melted just like the biscuit stinking, baseball cap wearing man in the post office. Some passed within a distinctive funk of their own special mix.

She lowered her eyes as far as she could whilst still being able to see her way clearly. Looking up at the departure board she scanned for the 14.06 to St Ives. Platform 14. Locating this at the far end of the station she headed for it with eyes still lowered, she noticed shoes of browns, blacks and the occasional red and even one green pair. There was a queue forming at the platform as the gate hadn't yet opened. Deciding against joining it, instead she took a step back and, propping up her case, waited on the sidelines away from the crowds.

She caught sight of those green shoes again. Quirky. A toilet shaped heel. With a huge buckle on the front and ribbon detailing. Very theatrical looking. The foot in the shoe was covered in crimson opaque tights.

The loudspeaker announced a short ten minute delay for the catering staff to restock. *Good* thought Mia her stomach rumbling. The last time she had taken this train with Alex there had been no refreshments available. They had shared an apple and a packet of salt and vinegar crisps on the six hour journey. It had been their own fault. Perry had invited them to someone's party and they had stayed way too late drinking until the early hours. They had woken late tired and hung over and had almost missed the train back to London. She was glad that Alex and Perry had got on so well. She was lucky that Alex had agreed she should go to Cornwall alone today. He could so easily have been jealous. Not that he had anything to be jealous about.

Maybe she could ask the interesting girl where she found her shoes. Her eyes moved up the crimson tights to a forest green wool coat. A huge peachy coloured flower corsage was displayed on the right shoulder. This was momentarily eclipsed by a huge leather jacket clad shoulder as the interesting girl was embraced by a man. He kissed her glossy hair and, as he pulled away, Mia caught a clear glimpse of the girl's tear filled brown eyes. *Or are they blue?* Mia felt breathless with a huge surge of love. He was going away. This was another of those all too familiar sad goodbyes, ten a penny at any train station or airport everyday the world over. Mia couldn't resist a look at the man as he let go of the woman. His eyes seemed unemotional. Not even a little mist within them at the sadness of the goodbye. Then the coal like black eyes stayed the same as his face started to melt.

Mia blinked hard and looked away. Looking back he had locked eyes with her now. She felt his coldness. She flinched at the ugliness of his mutating features. She looked again at the girl with the green shoes wondering if she knew that she would not be seeing this fake insincere man again.

Mia saw and felt that she did know. The force and flow of her tears would be fast and then forgotten. She smiled. Of course a girl with such exquisite taste in shoes knew that she was destined for something real not this fake excuse of a man. Resisting the urge to go across and tell her as much the crowd started to move forward slowly.

The train was now boarding. Those ten minutes seemed to have passed in a blink. Mia checked her ticket and kept walking on to carriage B at the front of the train. Climbing on board, she was one of the first in the carriage. She pushed her case in the luggage store and carried on down the aisle to find her seat putting her bag in the overhead shelf.

'Going somewhere?'

Turning around she took her seat opposite the owner of the voice.

'You've hurt yourself,' the woman continued, 'Come closer and let me see.'

Mia looked across the table between them as the woman took her hand.

'Honestly, it's nothing, it will heal,' she was visibly wincing now, 'Just a little burn from a hot baking tray it won't kill me.'

The kind looking old woman pulled Mia closer. Lifting the lid off the plastic box on the table before them she took out and opened a sandwich. Using her finger she spread some of the golden contents, which looked a lot like honey, on to Mia's hand. It never even crossed her mind to pull away. Their heads were close now, the old lady smelled of Parma Violets, her silvery purple rinsed hair almost touching red curls.

Mia lifted her head and cocked her ear to the low faint buzz that sounded like static. She noticed the woman's eyes were violet; as purple as the shawl that was draped around her small rounded shoulders.

More people started walking through the carriage, fixing their luggage and taking their seats. The woman spoke softly so that no one could overhear.

'Don't tell anyone what you are doing. Trust no one. And don't let anyone know what you are.'

Mia pulled away. For the first time in their encounter she felt slightly uncomfortable. She looked at the woman; she looked and smelt purple. Her bright sparkling eyes exuded wisdom. Nothing in her demeanor gave Mia any cause for concern. The lovely warm feeling she radiated was even strangely comforting.

'Do you want a lonely life?'

'Excuse me,' still slightly doubting her instincts, Mia needed a couple of minutes to think, 'I need the toilet.'

'No use of the toilets until the train departs the station,' bellowed the passing guard, 'Won't be long now' he added, addressing her personally.

Getting out of the way of the other passengers, she reluctantly sat back down.

'I don't think that will happen. I'm married,' she held up her wedding ring finger so that the old lady could see that she was wearing a wedding band, 'Two babies, so you see no time to be lonely.'

The old lady continued talking slowly. She chose her words carefully. She had a message for this young woman which she fully intended to pass on. 'Where are they now then? Take nothing for granted in this life. And beware the psychic vampires. Your aura is bright. They will tap into you. Use you up. They will bask in you. And leave you flat out, a shell. Remember this. Reject negativity. Or the blackness will trap you.'

The train whistle blew to the chugging motion of the train starting out of the station. Mia smiled politely. *What the hell was that all about?* She wasted no time getting up and, heading for the toilet, squeezed past some passengers standing in the aisle of the now packed carriage.

Closing the toilet door behind her she caught sight of herself in the mirror. Ready to splash water on her face she paused remembering the burn, not wanting to get it wet. Stunned she looked at her right hand. The burn was gone. It didn't make sense. Doubting herself, she double checked her left hand. Nothing. No sign of the burn.

Quickly she headed back to the carriage. All the seats were filled now. Only her reserved seat was vacant. She studied the faces searching for the old lady. A young good looking guy was sitting opposite her empty seat now. He looked puzzled when she asked him where the old lady was that was sitting there earlier. He pulled out an earphone from his right ear and shrugged. Looking around at the other passengers nobody said anything as they continued staring into space, reading or listening to their music.

13

The train finally pulled into the seaside town. Pushing the button the door opened with a whoosh and Mia stepped into the salty air, seagulls circling above. She spotted Perry immediately. She couldn't fail to as he came bounding towards her wearing a bright orange scarf. Embracing she breathed him in slowly, finding comfort in his lovely familiar scent. It was real; no man made scents of disguise just an all natural smell of him. Just him, with the smell of the sea and a quick splattering of rain for good measure, welcoming her arrival to Cornwall.

'Come on. Let me take you home and get you drunk!' he took her suitcase.

Ten minutes drive up a very steep hill and they were home and dry. He carried her bag up the stairs.

'I thought you would like this room, get you in the mood.'

She looked around taking in the shelves of books, potions and herbs, the real full size stuffed fox and the black raven hanging from the ceiling. Her amazed eyes met the large shining ball hanging in the window. A loud 'ri-bit' sound made her jump.

'That's my toad,' explained Perry 'Don't worry he's not poisonous.'

'Perry this room is like a movie set.'

'You'll be ok here. Protected. You'll sleep peacefully, you wait and see.'

She spotted the Ouija board laid out on the side table.

'What?' he read her troubled expression.

'They scare me Perry. Would you mind moving it for me please?'

'Course. Still it doesn't sound like you need that at all. Your channels are well and truly open. Have a good rest tonight and we can start work on fixing things in the morning. I made this for you.'

She took the effigy which was fashioned in wood and twigs and hugged him.

'I love it. What is it?'

'It's a mandrake man.'

The main body of the mandrake man was a tree branch, with legs and arms made from long twisted branches of the same tree. Its eyes were two shiny pieces of a jet coloured stone. Looking up, a similar one dangled on a piece of clear cord from the orange fringed light shade.

'I miss you being around so much. I don't know what I would do if I didn't have you to turn to. This is all just so weird.'

'Unpack. Come down when you are ready I'm making us something to eat. It's lovely to see you. You will be ok, you know.'

Unpacking didn't take long. She had done the travelling thing before settling down and she had learned then, the hard way, that she that travels lightest travels easiest. She hated any kind of heavy baggage, the emotional kind as well as the physical. She had known that her desire to explore had to be satiated before she could even think of settling down or having children. That had been a testing time for her relationship with Alex and resulted in them parting. They had lost touch completely. He couldn't understand her need to be free to explore life and what was out there but, even at that young age, she knew that she had to do it having the insight that it would be back to bite her on the ass again in a few years time. Then it would be too late as her life would take on a different shape and she would have other commitments and considerations that would stop her from following her dreams. It was the same in all aspects of her life. If she felt a stone needed to be upturned, she had to do it. Temptation always won and she always did so with the focus and braveness of a true adventurer. Upon her return Alex had pursued her for months until they were finally reconciled, him the same, her a very different woman from the one he had loved before.

She went downstairs. Perry loved to cook and he was good at it. They chatted easily as he finished cooking the meal. Mia felt at home, happy and loved in his company.

'I love your house Perry. It's so good to see you settled and happy here after everything.'

He poured her a glass of wine and went back to chopping some carrots. The smell of garlic filled the air.

'I grew these myself,' he held up a twisted misshapen carrot, 'Not the prettiest example, they taste better than they look.'

'I hope so!' she laughed.

'I lost heart at the other house. It was on the market for so long I didn't think it would ever sell. It was hell living there with Adam when the shit hit the fan. I love the peace I feel now. After all the arguments it was such a relief to find a buyer.'

'I know what you mean. We were so lucky with ours that it didn't drag on for too long but I did think we were gonna have to pull out on them at one point.'

'Moving is stress from start to finish. I hated showing people around. They come in and look at all your stuff. It's such an intrusion. One night this couple came. I got the impression they were brother and sister. They wanted to buy to let. They were looking to cash in. Wanted to know what we were leaving. They hadn't even put in an offer. Are you leaving the curtain poles? Are you leaving the curtains?' he scraped the home grown chopped vegetables into the griddle pan, 'Fucking silk curtains, Mia. I said no unfortunately they were not included in the price. But I told them that I would leave a turd in the toilet for them as a little house warming if they wanted to make an offer. No extra charge! Tight bastards. Looking for a fast buck out of other people's fucking misery.'

'So did they put in an offer?'

'Did they fuck! I don't ever wanna move again. Have everything I need here. That's why I try not to be too chummy with people here. One fucking weirdo and that's it, your peace is fucked. And you have to move again.'

Mia was reminded of Perry's penchant for profanities when he drank though he retained his beautifully sharp enunciation.

'You calling other people weird,' she smirked,

'that's really something.'

'That's what I mean,' he was smiling now, 'the least they know about me the better, in my opinion. And that goes both ways. They know I make my bits and sell them at the market but they just think I'm into Potter. I told one of them JK was a cousin once removed. It was a test to see how long it would take to get about. Next night out I had so many drinks bought for me and my ass was covered in kisses. I said didn't they know that writers are notoriously private people and I was disappointed that word had spread so rapidly. Ratted out their game, good and quick.'

Mia smiled. He had always had a way of sussing people out. It wasn't always a good thing, as she, cynical as it may be, believed most people work on ulterior motives and hate to be seen through. Even more so when their true colours are exposed with a well timed, whispered lie, as bait.

'I thought I was trapped in that old house forever,' Perry continued his tone becoming more serious, 'We couldn't sell the place. I thought, this is it, I have found my living hell. It was like I was trapped there, in some kind of vortex, not knowing why I couldn't break out. And Adam was still there, that was hell too. Who wants to carry on sharing a house with an ex. P-leease! I am not that fucking civilized. All hell was breaking loose. So the next viewers, I promised them it all. Fucking silk curtains. Car in the drive.'

'Turd in the jon!' added Mia.

They both laughed.

The smell of cooking filled the air 'Hey, we're gonna smell like a right couple of biscuits!' said Perry talking in shorthand with their code word for that lingering sweet cooking smell which hangs around some people.

Mia thought back to the day she had sent the letter telling Perry about this visit; the encounter in the post office with the biscuit baseball cap man.

'So what about you? I hear you finally got your house with the bush. 70 Hairy Mound.

'It's Harley Sound,' laughed Mia, 'but you got the number right. No excuse not to come and see us now.'

'No, I have two excuses now', referring to the kids, 'How was the birth? No on second thoughts, don't tell me. You are here. You survived. That's all I need to know,' he stirred the pan, 'Sounds like a venue for a biker's conference. Number 30 would have been a biker's meeting. Number 70 definitely makes it a conference.'

Perry was referring back to their first meeting. Mia had staged a mystic conference. He had been one of the exhibitors. They had clicked and kept in touch.

'A bloke living there before was a music producer biker.'

'That figures. The girl's done good. Why did they move?'

'The McKenzies split up I think. Usual thing, another woman, sent his wife Louise a bit doolally, so I heard.'

'Sent Lou-Lou loopy eh? Did he mention anything strange going on in the house?'

'Nothing on the forms.'

'Well I guess people don't really reveal stuff like that do they? Think they'll be judged and carted off for psychic examination. Bit like seeing a UFO, lot more of it about than you get to hear of. People worry other people will think they're mad. People worry too much about sanity. It's overrated. And it's easier to convince yourself it was all a dream anyway. Even if you know for sure that you weren't asleep.' Perry raised his eyebrows as he started to dish up the dinner.

Alex had driven to Pearl and Herb's straight from work to see the kids. Pearl had cooked. They had bathed the kids and then eaten together. From the moment he had met their daughter they had made him welcome in their life. He was lucky to have such good in-laws. He knew from friends and colleagues that wasn't always the case.

Driving home afterwards he felt lonely at the thought of going home to an empty house. He would get a bath and go straight to bed. Time passes in an instant when you are sleeping.

He rolled over to see Jayne seated on the bed. *What was she doing here?* He watched as she stood up before him, naked apart from silky panties. Her breasts were huge and unbridled, her skin the yogurt cream colour of a natural redhead. With a splattering of freckles. Fairy kisses. That was what Mia liked to call them.

Looking at the silken silver material Alex stared hard; it appeared to be moving. He strained to look in the near darkness. He watched as a solitary bluebottle edged and escaped from within the high cut crotch piece. Looking on in disbelief as Jayne started to sway, wiggling her hips in an enticing dance. The fly

was doing its own dance on its silver stage, its green
and blue armour glinting a mini light show in time to
its every motion.

Moving closer to Alex's face she hooked her
thumbs into either side of her knickers, and still
gyrating, she slowly peeled them down. Pushing him
backwards on the bed she sat astride him, kissing him.
Carried away in the moment, he started kissing her
back. She pulled at his pyjama bottoms. Pushing her
shoulders away from him he caught the outline of her
full rounded breasts.

Close up the freckles began to get fuller and redder
finally taking on the appearance of tiny rose bud lips.
They moved and pursed into a hundred tiny pulsating
kisses, covering her body. His eyes traced the curve of
her hip. Looking at her now in a full frontal pose, he
noticed the colour of her pubic hair. *Matching collar and
cuff.* It was bright orange. *With shiny electric blue and green
highlights?* Puzzled he watched as her rainbow
coloured mound began undulating and moving. He
was wide-eyed as the now pulsating mass erupted into
a swarm of flies, shocked as they bombarded his face
and chest, choking him. He let out a horrifying
scream, quickly flicking on the bedside lamp.

Suddenly everything was back to normal. The flies
and their amplified buzzing had gone. He looked at
Jayne's smirking face. He smiled letting out a sigh of
relief. She smiled a slow enticing smile back at him
slowly revealing rotting stumps for teeth. He blinked.
Frowning hard and blinking his wide eyes again and
again until she looked normal again. *Why was she here?*

'I can't do this!' getting up and grabbing his
clothes, 'This is not right!'

'Fool!' cackled Jayne as he watched her pass

through the door.

Now standing by the side of the bed, he looked down at his jeans. Inside out, the zip still open they felt strangely tight and he realized he was still wearing his pyjama bottoms underneath.

14

The following day Mia and Perry went exploring in the seaside town. A dream for Mia it was full of quirky gift shops, artist showing their handmade crafts and antique shops. They stopped outside one with a shining witch ball, just like the one Perry had, hanging in the window.

'This is the one,' said Perry opening the door for her. As they walked through a little bell tinkled their arrival.

Mia closed her eyes smelling the air. 'It smells old in here,' she whispered.

'What do you expect… it's an antique shop,' Perry tutted, rolling his eyes as he gestured to the witchball hanging in the window.

Towards the back of the shop was a doorway covered with a wooden beaded curtain. There were several old clocks in the shop. They tick-tocked an unsynchronized, repetitive, chorus. Mia detested ticking clocks with their never ending knell of time passing. *Why would anyone want to be reminded of that?*

'Good afternoon.' The beads gently swayed, knocking together as the shopkeeper emerged from behind them.

Mia and Perry nodded politely.

'I see you are admiring the ball.'

'Yes,' Mia replied her voice sounding so loud to her in the quiet, 'I have been looking for one.'

'She is not for sale I am afraid,' the shopkeeper spoke in a deep slow voice.

'Oh we thought as it was in the window.' Perry's humour was lost on the tall gaunt man standing before him.

'Yes. It is a witch ball. Folk do tend to hang them in the window.'

'Well,' Perry conceded, 'of course they do, how silly of me.'

Mia knew him well enough to know his heckles were up now at the shopkeeper's incorrect assumption of ignorance.

'Yes. Silly us,' she said in an effort to diffuse the sudden change in mood, 'Still, an easy mistake I guess.'

'Quite,' said the shopkeeper, tired of tourists and their ignorance, 'Please feel free to browse.'

'Thank you,' Perry asserted, his voice faster now, 'But it was the ball we were particularly interested in.'

'Like I said,' the shopkeeper's voice in turn sounding slower as he spoke clearly and deliberately, 'It is not for sale.'

Mia looked intently at the witchball, on tiptoe now, stretching up and looking at her own distorted reflection looking back at her. As she peered ever closer her features were contorting like looking in a hall of mirrors or into the back of a very large spoon.

'It belongs to my aunt,' the shopkeeper explained, 'She owns this shop. It has been hanging in that window for many years. Before that it hung in her family home. It has been in the family since she was a little girl and, I am told, indeed when her mother was also a girl before her. It is very old.'

'It must have seen many things,' said Perry, his voice softening now.

'Quite. It is rare. An original. No amount of money would make my aunt part with it.'

'No I understand,' said Mia, 'It must hold great sentimental value.'

The shopkeeper was on a roll now. He had not spoken to anyone but his aunt for days and, their interest piqued, he decided to be generous and enlighten them.

'They are protectors,' he went on, 'Well, of course, that is if you believe in that type of thing. Do you believe?' he delivered his question in the style of an old schoolmaster.

'Well I believe that everyone has to believe in something,' offered Mia. The man's voice was captivating and it occurred to her how wonderful it would be to have him tell her a bedtime story. She liked the way he was dressed; like he had stepped out of a very old black and white wedding photograph. Much like the one that hung on the wall next to one of the many time pieces, beating out their incessant reminders; death is always approaching knells.

A pissed off Perry remained quiet. His boredom threshold couldn't get any lower these days.

'It dates back to the 1800s. Maybe even before that. Legend has it that they protected the homes they hung in from evil spirits,' the shopkeeper watched as the red haired woman, eyes wide, hung on his every word. He paused for dramatic effect. 'Witches,' he continued in the style of an expert storyteller, 'Any evil that peers upon the ball will be reflected. And save the household of ills. Others go further and say that the reflected evil is trapped and so is the witch's soul. Trapped. Forever more. Within the ball.'

'God help anyone that drops one then,' said Mia tongue in cheek, immediately regretting it, she wished she could eat her words.

'Indeed.' The woman's off the cuff, flippant response had merely reinforced the accuracy of the label he had given them; ignorant of the old ways through and through. *God help them they know not what they do.* He continued, eager to get them out of the shop now. 'That person, that place, would be condemned to share their life with the evil they helped set free,' he was studying Mia intently now looking for a reaction, 'If you believe…that is.'

'We should go,' said Perry breaking the silence, he was tired of this macabre Jackanory session, 'Maybe we should keep looking.'

'Yes. Ok Perry, just one minute.' The shopkeeper was still looking at Mia as she searched inside her bag. 'I wonder if I might leave my mobile number,' she said taking a pen from her bag, 'I am only down from London for a few days. I was really hoping to find a witch ball to take back with me for my new house,' she scribbled her number on a scrap of paper, 'Maybe you would be kind enough to look out for another for me. I'd be very grateful.'

'As you wish,' said the shopkeeper taking the number from her.

The bell tinkled in the back office signaling their departure.

Catching up with Perry, Mia laughed.

'What?' he grinned, 'Scorn you may my lovely,' his voice taking on a high pitched Witchy Poo accent, 'but believe me you don't wanna be letting the anger and nastiness get the better of you around one of those things!'

'Peter,' a soft voice called from behind the bead curtain back at the shop.

'Coming Aunt,' said the shopkeeper.

'Call her back.'

'I will just as soon as we have one for her.'

'Call her now. She must have it.'

'What about the shop?'

'I have been expecting her. Call her. She needs it.' The silver haired old lady with the purple rinse was seated in a wheelchair, her legs covered in a crocheted blanket of purple and orange. 'Dear nephew, it's about time you realized, what are you now? Forty five? You should know by now that money isn't everything, my dear. What goes around comes around. Believe me. The girl needs it.'

'You can't even see her.'

'I don't need my eyes to see,' explained the old lady, her useless eyes as opaque as those of a cooked fish.

'What about the shop? The shop needs it. We need it.'

'Call the girl. Let me worry about protecting us.'

Peter looked at the scribbled number. Walking to the shop door he opened it and looked both ways to see if he could spot the two Londoners. They were nowhere to be seen. He screwed up the piece of paper and, flicking it into the street, he went back inside turning the 'open' sign over to 'closed'.

15

The three young men passed the joint around.

'We need some more readies,' said one of them pulling up his hoodie against the cold night.

Earlier they had pooled their limited resources in the offie; they had spent it all on beer which they were now drinking on the street corner.

'Pass us another tinny bro.'

'Nothing left. Here finish this,' he passed over what was left of the spliff.

'We need some money,' the hoodie repeated.

'There is no-th-ing here ma-an,' his mate spoke, nearly singing the words, in lilty, almost rhyming tones, 'I wan-na make me some mon-ey so I can get out-a this dive. Gonna get me up to Lon-don town. Find me my for-tune bro. I hear the streets are paved with go-ld!' the intonation of his words dancing up and down, as he delivered his impromptu poetic speech.

Stoned they all laughed and scoffed.

'Come on man,' said the obvious ringleader as the others followed.

They walked along the deserted street. Poet

Hoodie dropped his empty can and kicked it. It rattled along the quiet street, stopping and spinning like a tossed penny outside the antique shop, before clattering to a stop.

'What about this one?'

'Full of treasure,' added his mate in his best mock pirate accent, holding a hand over one eye as a makeshift patch.

'Full of old junk more like,' said the ringleader 'Come on you pair of pricks.'

Doing as he was told he followed Captain Hoodie for a second before changing his mind.

'Fuck you… you ain't my fucking dad!' said the Poet Hoodie under his breath as he looked up at the shop name *Florence Renata Bridgestock & Nephew*.

He was hungry; he wanted a kebab and another drink. He looked down at the can and crushed it beneath his top of the range trainer. He eyed them with relish, their orange piping vivid and crystal clear, he loved the clarity a toke gave him. Looking up his eye caught the large Christmas bauble in the window. It wasn't even Christmas yet. He giggled like a girl.

There looking back down at him was a face. He blinked. *Must be my reflection.* The deep penetrating bloodshot eyes stared back at him. *Shit I look rough.* As a slow smirk worked its way across the mouth the black eyes stayed focused on his. His stomach rumbled, the munchies fast approaching now. Then the pit of his moaning stomach fell away at the realization that HE wasn't smiling and this was no reflection. The black forked tongue lashed out making him jump in his skin. *Man that was good shit* he thought as he ran to catch the others up.

16

Perry's house was conveniently located near to The Bucket of Blood, a very old quaint looking local pub, full of local people. Mia walked in first. All eyes were suddenly on her as the background chatter fell silent. Hot on her heels they noticed Perry and the momentary silence was replaced by the quickly resumed conversations. Mia and Perry headed straight for the bar.

'How do Perry. The usual?' The landlady, glass in hand, was already at the pump pulling his usual.

Not that Perry considered he had a 'usual'; how conventional he thought saying nothing. 'Thanks Rita. This is Mia, remember I told you she was coming down from London for a few days?'

'And for you Mia my dear?' Rita said eyeing the stranger, 'What's your poison?'

'A white wine please Rita. Dry, thanks.'

Mia and Perry took the seats at the bar. They chatted, with Rita joining in between serving.

'We went into St Ives today,' Perry spoke between sips, 'Had a nosey around the flea shops.'

'The Bucket of Blood. What a great name, how did

it come about?' asked Mia.

'Legend has it that an old landlord was collecting water from the well out back to put with the hops to make the ale,' explained Rita speaking with a strong Cornish accent, 'Well this particular day, when he pulled up the bucket it was filled with blood. And a severed head!' laughing heartily seeing Mia shudder she continued, 'You should take her to The Blood Hound Perry. Nothing to do with those fox hunts, mind. Legend has it that the Canis lupus still guard the sight. Some of the locals have seen them. Frightened them near to death! Some have vowed never to set foot in the place again.'

'Canis lupus?' asked Mia, 'What's that then?'

'The Grey wolf. They say a local witch was having it away with the landlord. His wife found out. Some say that it is the very witch's head that was found in the well. She was never seen again you see.'

Mia was enthralled now waiting on the words which flowed from the full ruby mouth as red as the capillaries that chased their routes around the ruddy plump face, coated in peachy soft downy hair. Perry looked on slightly bored with another story he had heard many times before.

'But reports are the wolves are seen to this day,' the landlady continued her tale relishing the new pair of ears before her, hanging on her every word, 'Some say she beckoned them from hell to haunt the couple forever more,' she paused for dramatic effect 'It worked. They fled into the night! Never to be seen again!'

They didn't stay too long in the pub. It was difficult to talk as the locals were unused to strangers and flocked over to find out who this woman with

Perry was. They hadn't seen him with a woman before. In fact they hadn't really seen him with anyone. He was generally alone. Back at the house they sat now chatting easily as they sipped wine.

'Well do you think you may be under some sort of psychic attack?'

'I don't know? What are the signs?'

'How are your electrics? Lots of power cuts? Faulty TV, laptop, any unusual interference?'

'Not that I have noticed but I am not sure what is happening. There have definitely been some strange things.'

'Maybe not so plain Jayne has put a spell on you?'

'I think she is trying to put a spell on my husband more like.'

'Well, you fight it.'

'That's easier said than done,' Mia took a sip of wine, 'Anyway Alex is his own person. He's a grown man. If that's what he wants, he can have it. I won't stand in his way.'

'Don't you think that's a bit of a defeatist attitude?'

'Probably,' she shrugged.

'Where's your fight gone Mia?'

'That's the thing. I really don't know what I am up against. I can just feel it…something is not right.'

Perry walked across to the kitchen cabinet taking out an old style bottle with a cork stopper.

'This is for you,' he said passing it to Mia, 'When you get home find yourself some nails.'

'Nails?'

'You know, metal nails, the hammer into wood type. Put one in the bottle. And then piss in it.'

She began to laugh hysterically.

'Use a funnel.'

'What will it do?'

'It will stop you getting piss all over the bathroom floor!'

They laughed together, Mia temporarily forgetting her fear. She cherished Perry's ability to make her laugh and feel better. In that moment she remembered why she loved him and missed him so much.

'It will protect you from any bad vibes that are coming your way,' he continued, seriously now, feeling the intimacy and the strength of their very real bond. He didn't need the reminder to know that he missed her being around too.

Mia handled the bottle as she thought about it.

'Tomorrow, we'll do a meditation. So no more alcohol,' he instructed clearing the table, 'Let's do the dishes. Busy day tomorrow.'

They had risen early, eaten a light breakfast of scrambled eggs followed by a bracing walk along the beach which was not far from Perry's house. He walked most days, her breath quickening she was finding it hard to keep up. The salty wind was stealing the words they spoke; each was finding it difficult to hear. Mia's mouth felt contorted by the cold. She wanted to stop, just for a few minutes, to catch her breath. She followed him through the rock formation. Like a giant hag stone, the centre hollowed out by the ebb and flow of the sea. The tide was out and, as they stopped within, immediately the wind abated. He took out two bottles of water from his rucksack, offered her one and took a few swigs of the other.

He was lucky thought Mia. He had created his own

utopia. His cheeks rosy, contentment sparkled in his kind eyes. She felt the circulation returning to her mouth and could hear the words clearly now as she spoke them.

'It happens when I am asleep.'

'Sounds like hag phenomena. Fag hag phenomena,' he laughed then thought better of it, 'I know, I know, it's no laughing matter.'

'You had it?'

'Sure but not for a while,' he really had to stop himself, this was no time for Carry On innuendo, 'It's terrifying.'

'Made me scared to sleep. So what do you think it is?'

'There are plenty of explanations. Depends which one floats your boat. Don't think anything has been proven.'

The wind still howled, Mia's curls were blowing but it made no sound within the stone wall in which they stood.

'Well what do you think then?'

'I can't tell you what to think. I can tell you what the suggestions are. Scientifically it can be put down to dream sleep.'

'You don't go much on science, I know that much, what else?'

Perry was thinking about how much of his gleaned knowledge to share. His experience of sleep paralysis frightened him more than anything that had happened to him on a conscious level. To feel threatened whilst your body feels frozen and unable to move had felt very disarming.

She was looking at him now watching his mind ticking over. It concerned her more that he was obviously contemplating keeping something back from her, something to the best of her knowledge, he had never done before.

'Well? Have you decided?'

'Decided?'

'How much to tell me?'

'If you are sure you want to know.' His glazed over eyes seemed to rediscover their usual dewy sparkle indicating that he had and was ready to give her his full attention. She nodded. 'First, if, when, this thing happens again Mia you must not show fear,' he remembered that this would be difficult. It had taken him at least half a dozen times before he could contain his fright which had shot off the scale every time it happened. Still, she nodded, silently urging him to tell her all he knew so he continued, 'Embrace the feeling Mia, accept it, welcome it. Remember it is not real.'

'Well it feels real enough,' she resisted saying more.

'Some say that it is a visit from Incubus,' he paused, 'Incubus is a demon.'

'Go on,' she prompted.

'He comes to use the sleeping woman to fulfill his own urges,' she had not gone into detail about the nature of the nocturnal happenings but he was certain that there would have been a sexual element to them, even if she had chosen for whatever reason not to mention it.

'What urges?' she wanted him to validate her clear as glass memories. She had carried the feeling that she had been unfaithful to her husband, even as he slept beside her, the act had felt so real.

'I think you know that. It happened to you right?'

'Yes. At least it felt as real as you and I sit here

now,' she started to cry, 'I couldn't move. I couldn't scream.'

'Mia it wasn't real,' he wrapped his arms around her, 'Yes I believe that it happened. You know that it happened but it wasn't real. Not real like this is now. It was a psychic attack. It took you, well your body, when you were not there.'

'But I was there, I felt it,' she didn't look at him instead concentrating on the rise and swell of the ocean as it lapped the sandy shore.

'You weren't really there were you? If you had been really there, inhabiting your body, you would have been able to move and kick and scream.'

'I tried, I really tried,' she was calming down now just telling him about it for she had mentioned it to no one.

'It isn't uncommon you know, films have been made about it.'

She had seen movies and had tried to dismiss the acts as her subconscious manifesting recall or sparking her imagination.

'It happens to men too,' she decided not to ask had he experienced it as something in him betrayed that he had, 'She is known as Lilith or Lilitu. Some say that she is the demon female, some say that she is just Incubus in disguise taking on the form which will appeal to the sleeping victim. Our dreams betray us Mia. When we are sleeping we are at our most vulnerable. Some say that this is the time these demons come in and that they have the power to attach themselves to us, stealing our energy, feeding on it like the invisible, insatiable thieves, they are.'

She wondered if there was an escape. Not sleeping was not an option.

'Meet them Mia, as you must but disarm them with your strengths, your beliefs. Let them have what they want, give it to them without fight. You will wake up instantly. They charge up from your fear. They can take no pleasure without it. When you present no challenge and offer up what is yours to give they will evaporate.' He hugged her again, taking off his scarf he wrapped it around her neck. 'Come on, let's get you home.'

Stepping out of their temporary rock sanctuary the sound of the howling wind invading their ears immediately. They walked home without talking, each enjoying the accelerating wind whistling around their bodies blowing the cobwebs away.

Later they sat in the living room, the heavy velvet curtains blocking out the cold bright day. Mia sat on the wooden floor watching as Perry lit some incense and the white pillar candles dotted about the room. He sat opposite her on the floor. Picking up the remote control he pointed it and the sounds of Rozalla's 'Are you ready to fly' began pulsating in the wispy, intoxicatingly sweet, air. Mia breathed deeply, exactly as he had told her to during their earlier walk.

Watching as he closed his eyes, she took her cue and did the same. In the candle lit blackness, she was aware of her breathing, of Rozalla's beautiful voice as she belted out the words which fitted the moment like a couture dress. As she listened the words and smell of the incense began to retreat as the colours in her tightly closed eyes began shifting and changing like a rainbow, until these too disappeared into a bursting fireworks display of shooting stars.

17

Without Mia and the kids the house felt too quiet to Alex. Especially at night; he wasn't used to sleeping alone. Tossing and turning in the too large bed, his restless sleep was interrupted by an annoying itchy nose. Unsure if he was dreaming he scratched and twitched. His ears were filled with a buzzing sound. He remembered that he had left the window open. *Damn fly.* Stirring now he shook his head in annoyance unaware of the fly as it crept from within his left nostril, aware only of the slight tickling sensation. As the solitary fly took flight, within seconds the swarm that followed it woke him. He couldn't breath! The buzzing in his ears, growing now to a frightening crescendo, filling his head, which felt like it might explode.

It was a dream. He exhaled in relief, the buzzing sound now replaced by quiet. Shaking his head he pushed back the covers and went to the en suite bathroom. Lifting the toilet seat he took a leak. He flushed but left the toilet seat up like he used to when he lived alone, enjoying the pathetic small act of defiance in his wife's absence. As he washed his hands, he looked at himself in the mirror. Sniffing he rubbed his nose. Feeling like there was something up there he grabbed a tissue. He raked around in there picking his nose with all the abandon his enforced solitude allowed. As he ripped out a massively loud fart his quick to kick in juvenile brain congratulated himself on the hat trick. Living alone definitely had some good points. Mia had 'refined' him as she put it, without saying anything, her looks of revulsion were enough, they spoke louder than any words. Her initial laughs at his monumental gas emissions had long since stopped. Laughing aloud now they still amused him. And little Grace too, when they too were on their own.

He was missing the kids. He was missing the noise and the chaos even though he was guilty of complaining about it. He heard the telephone start ringing. Throwing the tissue down the toilet he went to answer it so he didn't notice as the tissue began absorbing the water or the shiny black fly now skating on the surface. Seated on the bed he smiled to hear Mia's voice and the news that she was on her way home. He missed her. Distracted with the excitement of her calling he flicked the fly away as it bombed passed his ear.

He got ready quickly, washed up the dishes now piled high in the sink (*hat trick plus one what's that called?*) and went to collect the kids. He was waiting for Mia to phone again so that they could all go to the station to pick her up when he heard a car pull up outside. Looking out he saw her getting out of the taxi as she paid the driver and wheeled her case up the path. Turning her key in the door she noticed Grace running up the stairs being chased by a grey dog.

'Grace,' taking off her coat, she called after her little girl.

'Hello Mummy,' Grace called between giggles, without stopping.

Miffed, Alex was back sitting in the kitchen reading the paper.

'I thought you were gonna call from the station? We were all looking forward to picking you up.'

'Sorry I saw the cab rank there and thought it would be easier,' she flicked on the kettle, 'Where's Ben?'

'Afternoon nap. Before I forget something came for you whilst you were away, special delivery. It's quite heavy, I left it in the garage.'

'Grace didn't even come and say hello,' opening her case Mia started to load the washing machine with her dirty laundry, 'I guess she is too busy with her new dog! Great Alex. I go away for a couple of days and you get her a dog. I don't want her getting everything she wants Alex! I need you to stand by me.'

'Hey?' said Alex looking up, puzzled.

His annoyance now subsiding he walked across to greet his wife properly. The sea air had done her good. She had some colour back in her cheeks. Or maybe that was from the steam currently coming from her ears. He had missed her. He had missed her fire! She shrugged off his embrace.

'I am pissed off Alex! Are you gonna be here to feed it and walk it. What were you thinking? And those ones are hardly known for being good with kids!'

'Well I kinda figured that Grace would deal with that.'

'What? Have you lost all sense of responsibility? She is only three years old.'

'Yeah and it's ok Mia. Lots of three year olds have imaginary pets. It helps them learn. It's great for kids.'

'Imaginary?'

Convinced he had done nothing wrong he smiled and started nuzzling up to his wife. 'Yes of course. I missed you. Have some faith in me Mia. I am hardly gonna add a dog to the mix. You have enough on your plate already, I do know that.'

'Do you know what type it is?

'Type?'

'Breed Alex. What kind is it?'

'I don't know. The imaginary kind. I didn't ask. Doubt she's decided yet and it'll probably change every day anyway. I guess it'll be a Westie. A white one. Now she knows they don't come in pink. That's what she wanted, eh. Why don't you ask her?' He gave up trying to schmooze his wife deciding instead to make them some coffee.

'It's a Grey wolf.'

'No way!' he laughed, then noticing her stern face, 'So you did ask her? I would've thought she would've gone for a pink Westie or maybe a pink poodle.'

'I am serious Alex,' she said, 'I saw it.'

He let the conversation go. He was watching his wife crumble before his eyes. Clearly going away had done nothing to help. He felt secretly glad that the all round good egg Perry had also failed where he had; it made him feel justified and less useless. She went off to have a bath. He had some work to do anyway. This called for the ostrich approach; he would keep his head down until it passed. Nothing he could do. It was just a matter of time it would blow over.

He was sat at the table working on his laptop when Grace came over and sat on his lap.

'Have you seen Mummy?'

'Yes she is having a bubble bath.'

'Why didn't you come and see her when she came home?'

Grace didn't answer.

'You knew Mummy was coming back didn't you. We told you she was just going to have a sleepover with her friend, like you did at Nanny and Grandad's.'

'I know Daddy,' she paused, 'But I was playing with my doggie and I thought Mummy would tell me off and send him back.'

Alex started an internet search of dog pictures.

'What dog is it Grace?' he asked scrolling through the pictures on the screen, 'Is it like this one?' he repeated, over and over, as he clicked on the many images as Grace kept shaking her head.

'No Daddy,' she finally said in frustration, 'Canis lupus.'

'What was that Grace?' He asked his daughter to repeat what she had said; the words he thought he heard were too complex to be uttered by such a tiny mouth. She repeated the words and he typed them.

The search engine offered the question 'Did you mean Canis lupus?' Clicking on the correct spelling another picture sprang across the screen.

'That one Daddy.'

Alex's brow furrowed as he studied the photo of the Grey wolf.

The next day was Sunday. It was sunny so Alex had suggested they all get their wellies on and go for a long walk in the nearby forest. He knew that Mia loved to walk and he hoped that it would clear both their heads. So they got wrapped up in coats, hats and gloves. Alex found the football under the stairs. Ben was still a bit too little but he couldn't wait to start having kick abouts with his son.

They walked along the paths through the tall canopies of trees, taking it in turns to hold Ben or hold his hand as he tried to keep up on unsteady legs. They came upon an open area and whilst Alex started kicking the ball lightly with the children, Mia took a few minutes on her own.

She breathed in the smell of the forest. The damp earthy scent was one of her favourite smells. She studied the different trees. Oak. Silver birch. Sycamore. They were all here and more. Hearing a rustling, she spotted a squirrel watching it run expertly up one of the trunks. She noticed the fairy pillow mushrooms growing on some of the barks. Another trunk was half hollowed out as it had split apart with growth and she couldn't resist looking inside and breathing in the earthy scent tinged with a whiff of wild mushroom.

She could hear the distant laughter of her family. Turning in their direction she caught sight of another tree. Its stubby short trunk had split into two branches which grew upwards tall and spindly. It reminded Mia of the mandrake man Perry had given her. It looked just the same albeit on a larger scale and upside down with its head buried in the soil.

Stepping back to admire it she noticed Grace was standing next to her. Without saying a word the little girl started to skip on the spot, arms slightly splayed, clenched hands seemingly holding an invisible skipping rope. *So much energy.* Mia smiled and watched as the jumping stopped with a jerk only to be replaced by a little run.

Grace was running now, around and a round in a circle, in the middle of which stood her mother. Faster and faster. Giggling. Faster and faster. Her daughter came in and out of focus as she ran around and around her. The minutes passed. Mia was dizzy. *She'll stop soon, she's only having fun, she'll get giddy too, soon.* Only her daughter didn't stop running. Around and around. Faster and faster. Mia's eyes blurred. In the smudged streaks of her daughter's red coat, its material splattered with a sprinkling of coloured stars, she thought she had seen the tip of a tail.

I like this game! Grace chased the tail around and around, giggling, louder and louder.

Mia felt the little girl's energy swirling around her. *Around and around she goes.* The coloured stars were moving ever faster, spinning like shooting stars across the blanket of the forest's green backdrop. Her daughter was stirring up her aura, invading it, strangling it with her invisible coiling trail, creating a vacuum, a vortex. *I can't breathe! Stop! Stop! I can't breathe.* Instinct kicked in with her over exaggerated lifted of her legs, one swiftly followed by the other, stepping up and over the invisible boundary of energy and stepping out of the circle.

She heard Ben scream. As she ran across to see what had happened she saw the little white furry bundle turn on its heels.

'You should keep your dog on a lead!' shouted Alex.

Mia thought she caught sight of the wolf as it reared at the little white dog causing it to yelp and run away in defeat.

'What did you do to my little dog?' the well dressed woman demanded, 'What did he do to you Tooty?' She was holding the little white poodle in her arms now, kissing and comforting it as she screamed, 'You keep away from us!'

Ben was crying. Grace patted the wolf on the head and it disappeared.

'What happened?' Mia was back with them.

'Oh nothing. The little dog got excited seeing the ball. It startled Ben. Ran off when he cried. The woman's mad. Did you see it? She had dressed it in one of those doggie jumpers. It even had a diamante collar. Please.'

'You ok Ben?' Mia took him. He was giggling again. 'Grace did you see the doggie?'

'Yes Mummy, it was wearing a jumper, silly.' Grace ran off again chasing the ball.

'Talk about overreacting!' said Alex.

As they walked past the 'buried mandrake' tree Mia decided against pointing it out to him. She looked back at it over her shoulder to take another look.

She thought she saw the wolf relieving itself against it.

18

Heading back to the house, they turned into their road slowing down to pass a neighbour. Funny thought Mia; Mildred usually waved or smiled at least. This time she merely looked away as Alex drove on before pulling into their drive.

'Ignorant cow!' he scoffed.

'Must be having a bad day.' Mia was feeling more charitable and still slightly shocked that her husband had even noticed the strange snub.

Back inside he offered to make some lunch. She collected all their muddy wellies and started to brush them off with a bucket of soapy water in the garage. Noticing the brown cardboard box she stopped. In the fuss and confusion of the 'imaginary' dog she had forgotten all about the package, taking a key she sliced through the brown tape.

She had found it online. The bubble wrap popped randomly as she split open the packaging to reveal the majestic looking face. It was larger than she imagined, expertly carved in some sort of clay or concrete. She traced its curved horns with her fingers. Something moved.

Shit! It had been broken in transit. She picked up the pieces of the right horn. Peering closer she noticed that the horn at the top of the head had also been misplaced. Pieces of stray stone were embedded in the gargoyle's staring eyes causing them to twinkle.

'Hello my name is Mia,' carefully picking out the debris, 'Welcome to my home. Looks like you had a bumpy ride.'

'Who are you talking to?' Alex came in, 'What is that?'

'It's a gargoyle.'

'You don't say,' he took a closer look 'What are you trying to do, scare the children? And me!' then looking at his wife, 'And you were talking to it!'

'I am going to get you fixed up.' Yes she was talking to it and she continued to even with Alex watching.

'Send it back Mia. It's beyond repair look at it. And it'll scare the kids. Those things shouldn't be inside they belong on churches.'

'He's old. He's a one off. I'll find someone to mend him. He probably was on a church once.'

'They were designed to frighten off evil Mia. Anything nasty that saw them would be frightened off and not even think of entering where they hung. If you believe that is.'

Alex's turn of phrase took her back to the old antique shop. That was exactly what the shopkeeper had said about the witchball.

'Exactly,' said Mia, 'They also had a practical use, drainage, you know. His job sat up on high in the church turrets would've been to let the water run through his open mouth. What's for lunch?'

'Tomato soup.'

'Oh good my favourite.'

'I know.'

'My perfect day, a walk in the woods followed by tomato soup.'

'And a delivery of an ancient gargoyle with devil horns, what more could a woman ask for?'

'Nails'

'What for?'

'Curiosity killed the cat. I just need some nails, big ones.'

'They are on the top shelf,' Alex said quickly losing interest, 'Don't be long I'm gonna put the soup on.'

Wondering through towards the kitchen he noticed the faint smelt of tobacco. Not the overwhelming clinging smell of modern cigarettes but the more subtle lingering earthy smell of his old granddad's brand. *Was it tobacco or was it incense?*

His memory sliced back to visits to churches when he was much younger - enforced visits that had put him off religion for life. He was lucky that Mia had felt indifferent and for that reason they had married without planning and without shoes with sand between their toes. The sweet smell may well have been the lingering remnants of the woody sap. It was one or the other; or maybe it was both. It smelled just like Jayne's house had.

Funny how people's houses all have their own unique aroma. Not the horrid fake plug in smells that, thankfully, Mia also detested. Nor the artificial spray of aerosols that polluted and masked the air. He, like everyone else, was used to the smell of his own abode. As he prepared the lunch, he wondered how their home smelt to others?

A few times recently he was sure that he had

detected the smell of dirty dog. A pungent heavy smell seemed to hang in the air, then seemingly disappear in front of his nose, as he walked around the house sniffing, rather in the fashion of a dog himself. Nothing. He hadn't mentioned it to Mia; she filled their home with freesias and scented aromatherapy candles depending on her mood. He had secretly welcomed Pearl's mentioning of the doggie smell one day, although he had of course, dismissed it as probably the myrrh that Mia had started using in her ceramic diffuser. He wouldn't really be able to recognize frankincense or myrrh and cared for neither though he had just let Mia get on with it; anything to keep the peace at the moment.

Later in the kitchen they all sat around the table enjoying their soup. Mia watched her daughter dipping her bread, her lips now looking big and clown like stained with orange.

She suddenly had a thought and getting up, went across to the wildlife food cupboard. There was only one solitary tin of dog food left. She had stocked up on it just before she went away. Alex would never feed the fox, he said it went against nature. Saying nothing, she grabbed some more bread and sat back down, catching her daughter's eye and hearing her soft childish voice telepathically 'I had to feed the fucking dog'.

19

Perry had a restless night when Mia left. After a couple of months living alone her presence shone a flashlight on to what was missing from his life. He had always found her company easy but the short stay had seen them grow even closer. After all the hassles with Adam he had come to associate company with power struggles and constant draining arguments. Mia had served as a reminder to him that it didn't have to be that way. There had been times during her visit when they had been quiet in each other's company and comfortable with it. Not that awkward silence. No it was a profound feeling of peace borne of mutual respect that can only exist amongst equals.

The lonely space she left had kept him awake. He had wondered what it would be like to be straight. Mia had often said that he was almost her perfect man. He would have loved to believe that. They were physically so different. He was slightly short and, as she had termed him, cuddly. The only other physical attribute they shared was a head full of curls. Hers were red, of varying shades it would seem each time he saw her. His was black with a sprinkle of grey; salt and pepper getting heavier on the salt with each passing day. She was tall and willowy but for her goddess hips, slightly bottom heavy if he were to be picky, what those fashion magazines would call pear-shaped. He only saw the arty curves of her feminine form so different from the outline of a man. He had drawn her once. And made a small goddess style clay image of her, whose vastly over exaggerated hips had caused her to scream playfully at him for his cheek. He had explained without irony that he had merely played on her best feature. He could appreciate the female body. What a tragedy it was that he could not have loved this woman as she had wanted to be loved. They were soulmates of that he was sure.

He stopped daydreaming. She was a wife and mother now. She had fulfilled her womanhood as nature had intended. He had to admit, but for the current weirdness that was invading her life, she seemed very happy. Only the vertical frown mark between her eyes at the top of her nose betrayed the worries that troubled her. He had sensed that she was uneasy but, like her, he was unsure how things would unfold. He had lain awake for nearly an hour now, thoughts turning over and over in his head.

Getting up he put the kettle on stupidly wishing she were still there to share a coffee with. He couldn't understand it. He would do anything to avoid other people first thing, especially until, as he liked to put it, he had his face on straight. It was taking longer these days for the pillow imprints on his face to plump up and his face to fall back to its natural contours fighting its never ending battle with gravity. Conversation first thing was a no no for anyone that knew him. He was best given a wide berth. Mia was different though.

There was something else on his mind. He had
dismissed it several times but it would not go away
and leave him be. The last thing he wanted was
another trip in to town. It would be crowded with
holiday makers. He simply wasn't in the mood. Yet
the thought niggled away. He knew that he had to go
back to the antique shop he had visited with Mia. He
didn't know why but he knew better than to ignore
these hunches. Maybe they had got something he had
wanted in stock. It had happened before when he had
a strong urge to go some place there was inevitably a
reason that soon made itself clear when he got there.
So he resigned himself to the trip and the feeling
temporarily subsided as he ate his breakfast in peace.

He took the train. Parking would have been
murder today, especially as the sun had made a grand
appearance. He wandered along the lane towards the
shop, suddenly kicking himself that he would be more
than pissed off should the shop be closed. Not that
he had ever seen it closed during any of his visits. Not
just those few he had made since he had lived here
but in all the times that he had holidayed here in the
years before. The shop had always been here. And the
shopkeeper had always been there. And he had always
looked old. Perry suspected that he was nowhere near
as old as he looked. He was one of those people that
looked as though they had been born old. That and
his sense of old style had added years that his unlined
face, on closer inspection, did not uphold.

Noticing the 'open' sign, Perry was glad as he
pushed open the door and stepped inside to the
familiar tinkle of the little bell. The old shopkeeper
was there. He looked up but showed no sign of

recognizing Perry from just days ago. Perry nodded and started to look around the shop, unsure of why he was there. There was no new stock. Everything looked the same as it had when Mia had been here with him. The witchball still took pride of place, shining, in the window.

Peter busied himself looking through accounts, dusting random items of stock, anything to avoid striking up a conversation again with the uncouth Londoner. His aunt was out back and would recognize the voice immediately as 'that chap that was with the woman that needed the ball'. She had not questioned him about it again, assuming that her instruction to call the woman back had been done. Perry felt uncomfortable and foolish as he headed for the door.

'Thanks I had a feeling you may have something for me, I was just passing. See you again.'

That did it. The old lady's ears pricked up in instant recognition.

'Peter! Peter! Is Perry here to collect the ball for her?'

Hearing the mention of his name, uttered by an unknown female voice too, caused Perry to pause and turn around.

'I thought your face looked familiar.' Peter was fooling no one. Least of all Perry, who was watching and waiting for the owner of the soft but authoritative voice, to emerge from behind the beaded curtain. She didn't.

'Yes Aunt. It's all in hand.'

Perry watched in quiet amazement as the shopkeeper walked across to the window, taking with him an old wooden low set of step ladders. He reached up and unhooked the chain, stepping back down carefully. He rested the witchball on a tapestry padded chair not far from the counter as he reached down and retrieved a box and some bubble wrap. He looked at the ball as if to bid it a silent goodbye, before wrapping it carefully with the protective popping plastic and finally placing it in the box, which he pushed with obvious reluctance towards Perry.

'For your friend,' the shopkeeper spoke without emotion, 'With the compliments of my aunt.'

Perry was stunned. Firstly at the about turn of the shopkeeper and also at the hunch that had brought him here again today. He finally spoke 'Thank you.'

'Make sure she is aware of the power it has.' The shopkeeper spoke with a poker face.

Perry thought it best to get out quick before he changed his mind. With no sign of the woman emerging, he leaned across the counter slightly and projected a slightly louder 'thank you'.

He headed towards the post office before deciding quickly not to risk the witchball being broken in the post. He would drive it to Mia. Surprise her with it. *Perfect.*

20

Mia heard the doorbell. She wasn't expecting anyone. Alex had just taken the kids to drop them off on the way to work and she had planned a 'Mia' morning. She checked her reflection. She looked a sight. Her hair was all over the place. *Shit!* Whoever it was could see her through the coloured glass of the front door. The soldier maneuver of dropping to the floor and crawling on her elbows out of sight as she had done on many occasions was not an option. Ignoring the caller was out of the question today. So, resigned, she put on a smile as she opened the door, maybe it would be Alex forgetting his key.

'Open up! Open up Mia I know you are in there!'

Mia stopped chastising Alex in her head when she heard the female voice. 'What's going on Mildred? What on earth's happened?' Mia stepped back opening the way for her neighbour to come in; she didn't.

'You have to be kidding.'

'What?' said Mia, 'Mildred whatever is the matter? Please keep it down, there's no need to shout.'

'Oh yeah,' Mildred ignored the request instead

bellowing, 'When it suits you. You don't like being disturbed yourself do you, sod everyone else though!'

'Mildred please keep your voice down.'

'Your dog is left out all hours, all weather, barking. Well I've had enough!'

'Dog? You must be mistaken Mildred.'

'Mistaken?! No! You need to do something about this, we've put up with this for long enough!' She had taken her voice down a couple of decibels but it was still much higher and shriller than the tones Mia had heard her neighbour speak in before.

'Please Mildred. We don't have a dog. You must be mistaken. Really. Come in and calm down. We can talk this through.'

Mildred stared back. The seconds passed slowly, without words and Mia wondered what on earth was happening.

'Why would you lie like that?' Mildred finally spoke 'Are you ill?'

'Ill?' Mia screwed up her nose and looked side to side wondering the same about her neighbour; was this woman for real and just what was her problem? A little laugh escaped Mia's pursed lips.

That was it Mildred erupted, her red lips exploding a torrent of cascading abuse. 'Don't laugh at me!' she momentarily regained her composure 'Wipe that smirk off your face.' She was very well spoken. Mia grinned, with a strange mixture of amusement and nerves, upon hearing the fuck expletive spoken with such crystal clear diction and in such a beautifully crafted rich accent. 'You,' Mildred paused 'Are a fucking weirdo.' She seemed to have double spaced between her words.

Mia was transfixed in her confusion.

'I saw you,' Mildred went on 'In the car.'

'Yes. And I saw you,' Mia said, this was too weird now.

'What is wrong with you woman?'

Was that a serious question thought Mia. Should she answer? She didn't really want to provoke her neighbour again so she looked and listened, intrigued as to what she was going to say next.

'Your fucking loud…fucking barking all day…fucking pain in the ass dog was in the fuck…king car!' There it was again, four fucking perfectly formed double spaced fucks coming from this clearly mad woman seeing and hearing things that weren't there.

'You are mistaken,' said Mia 'I really must go now.' She quietly closed the door. *Fuck, she can see it too*.

There was another bang at the door. What more could she say to the woman? Denial wasn't working.

Mia put on her Eleanor Rigby smile again. The fake smile was quickly replaced with a genuine beam as she saw Perry standing there.

'Perry! You came.' She was happy to see him and happy that it wasn't Mildred ready for round two.

'I come bearing the gift of silver,' he said presenting her with the box.

'Well you haven't come all that way just to deliver that, come in!' she said excitedly grabbing her friend and almost pulling him inside, forgetting quickly about the dog and Mildred.

'What is it? Oh it is so good to see you! Where is your luggage? How long are you staying! Will you stay for Grace's party?!' She bombarded him with questions.

'Steady on. I wasn't planning on staying. Just had

to get this to you safe. Wasn't worth the risk of it getting smashed in the post.'

'You drove all this way to deliver this. You are a sweetheart. Mad too I have to say.'

'Shut up,' interrupted Perry, 'and open it.'

Mia ran the edge of the scissors along the brown tape. Opening the box, she started to tear open the bubble wrap, enjoying the noise of the occasional pop. Peering in she noticed her own face, distorted like in a fairground hall of mirrors, staring back at her.

'You found me a witch ball!'

'Not just a witch ball. It's THE WITCHBALL.'

She took hold of the rusty metal chain and pulled the ball from its protective packaging.

The friends, seated at either side of the table, studied their own distorted reflections in the shiny silver ball, spinning slightly on the chain, as it hung between them.

'Oh look,' said Mia, 'It's a bit damaged.'

'Where?'

She pointed to the small area at the bottom of the arc where the silver was slightly worn away.

'Are you kidding!' Perry mocked, 'Do you know how old this is? It's not modern repro. Look at the mottling and the bubbling. And look at the stopper. And the chain.'

The chain was quite rusty. Mia felt the coolness and smoothness of the ball.

'I know. How did you persuade him to sell it to you? It must have cost a lot.'

'I didn't,' said Perry deciding not to go into details of how he came to be in the shop again, 'They insisted. Well it seems the aunt did. I didn't buy it Mia. She insisted you have it.'

'Really?' said Mia, 'How strange. How kind too. What is she like?'

'I didn't see her. But she insisted you must have it.'

'I must write her a thank you.'

'There's the shop address.' Perry pointed to the stamp on the side of the box. *Florence Renata Bridgestock & Nephew.*

'How old do you think it is?' She was thinking aloud as she ran her fingers over the knobbly slightly raised area of imperfection.

'Early 1900s I would say. It's the real deal Mia. Look after it.'

'I wonder what it has seen?' As she spoke she moved her face backwards and forwards making her features get bigger and smaller as she did so. Perry did the same on the opposite side of the table and they collapsed in a fit of giggles. Composing themselves they became serious again.

'I wonder if it's real,' said Mia, 'I wonder if there really is anything in there?'

'I for one would rather not find out,' shuddered Perry, 'Where are you going to hang it?'

Mia thought for a minute looking around.

'Over the patio door I think.'

'Do you have a hook? I could do it for you now before I go.'

'Oh why don't you stay Perry? See Alex and the kids.'

'No I won't today Mia. I said I'd call in on the family on the way back. Break the journey.'

'That's a shame,' she was disappointed, 'It was really good of you to bring it. A lovely surprise to see you. I didn't expect that, especially so soon. I think I have a hook.' Mia looked in the drawer.

'It'll have to be secured in the lintel.'

'Do you think the chain will be long enough? The ceilings are quite high. I think I'll wait and see if Alex has anything in the garage to extend it.'

'Ok. Well I am going to love you and leave you.'

After a quick tour around the house, Mia waved goodbye as Perry left as quickly as he came.

Later when the kids were in bed, she showed Alex the witchball.

'What is it? It looks like a giant Christmas bauble.'

'Yes, I suppose it does. It's antique. People used to hang them in their windows to ward off evil spirits.'

'Really? Takes all sorts I suppose,' dismissing the hocus pocus of the idea, 'Still if you like it, that's all that matters.' His house was fast becoming home to all sorts. Still if it kept Mia happy he supposed that was all that mattered.

'Will you hang it for me? I found a hook but I want it to hang a bit lower. The chain is a bit short. Do you have anything in the garage?'

'I'll have a look,' thinking what he might have that would do the job, 'I think I have something in the car,' he remembered the bit of old belt, it would be ideal. 'I'll go and look.'

He went out to the car. Rooting around in the back he found the chain, on the floor, from Jayne's car that she'd given him the day it had got stuck. He thought back to that day. It was all so innocent. He wished he had mentioned it to Mia. He hadn't kept it from her deliberately, merely forgotten it as it had slipped his mind. The chain was old looking. Jayne had produced it from her boot the only thing she had to offer, it was too puny and weak to pull a car. He thought at the time that she knew this and was overdoing the damsel in distress routine a bit. It wouldn't look out of place holding Mia's latest weird purchase though. He wondered if Jayne was missing it and if he should take it back. Taking a pair of heavy pliers he snipped off a few chains. He was sure that Jayne wouldn't want it back, it was broken anyway. He only needed a short piece. Going back in the house he showed it to Mia.

'Is this ok? I can pick something up tomorrow if you don't like it but you don't want anything too shiny and new or it will look out of place.'

'No that looks perfect.'

Alex fixed the hook in as Mia secured the chain to the ball. She wanted to hang it herself so he stepped down off the chair and passed the witchball to her and she slipped it on to the hook.

'Be careful with that hook. We should have used a closed loop hook really. If that is knocked at all, it could swing off that hook, I'll look out for one.'

She stepped down and back to admire it. She liked it. Its shiny surface added light to the kitchen.

'Looks good. Thanks Alex.'

He had gone for a shower so, finding some notepaper, she sat down to pen a thank you letter to the shopkeeper's aunt. She wrote their address and started to compose the letter. Dear. She stopped. How should she address the woman? She didn't know her status. The shop name held no clues. Dear Madam sounded so formal. Dear Florence too familiar. Was she a Miss or Mrs Bridgestock? She wanted to make sure the thank you hit the right note. It would be so easy to cause offence; this lady came from an age of manners and etiquette. She settled on Dear Florence Renata Bridgestock. A little formal perhaps but it was respectful. Keeping it brief she made the tone of the rest of the letter friendly. She signed off with assurances that the witchball would be treasured and well looked after. She would post the thank you letter first thing.

21

In the garage Alex looked at the gargoyle. He wondered should he interfere with the head or let Mia fix it herself. His chance meeting with Jayne had been a great coincidence not to be missed. She was obviously an expert and would do a far better job. He would get the hideous head restored to its former glory. It would be a nice surprise for Mia and save her the trouble. Loading the concrete cast with the broken bits into the boot he set off for Jayne's. She was in the garden.

'Hello Alex what can I do for you this fine day?'

'Actually, you may be able to help me with something. Mia asked me to pick up something to fix a broken ornament.'

'What's it made of?'

'Concrete. It's a…' Alex paused before adding, 'A sort of garden ornament.'

'Have you brought it with you?' she followed him across to the car, 'I'll take a look at it for you. Is this the casualty?' she said as he opened the box to reveal the head.

'Yes do you think you can fix it?'

'Doddle!' they both laughed, 'Not just any old garden ornament then?'

'Mia bought it online. From some church I think. Not my kind of thing really.'

'It's a gargoyle.'

'Um I know what it is. And what they are for. Drainage.'

'Um. Leave him with me. The break will need time to set. He'll be outside in the courtyard so you can collect him whenever it suits you, anytime from tomorrow. I'll get the break cemented today. It'll be done. Nothing will undo it once I have set it.'

'Do you think you'll still be able to see the damage?'

'I'll do my best to disguise and hide the break Alex. But if you look close enough you'll see the cracks. If you know what you are looking for and the cracks are there you never have to look too closely to see them…once the cracks are there, they'll always be there.'

'Well if you can do your best work, I'll be grateful.'

'Like I say damage is hard to fix once it's been done but I will get in between the cracks.' She closed the box flaps resealing the brown tape securely and he carried the heavy box across to the house.

He was about to follow her inside with it.

'Leave it outside Alex, just on the patio table will be fine.'

Placing it on the garden table he followed her into the kitchen. He noticed the spider sitting in its web; it had chosen to spin its home in the small alcove between Jayne's range and the wall. He wondered had she spotted it? It was large with long hairy legs and tiny eyes on stalks.

'You have seen that?' he gestured in not so Itsy Bitsy's direction.

'Yes of course,' Jayne continued dismissively.

'I could get rid of it for you? If they give you the creeps I mean?' offered Alex.

'That won't be necessary thank you Alex,' she laughed, 'That's her home. Have you seen the work that goes into spinning those webs?'

'Mia would freak.'

'Well,' Jayne chose her words carefully, 'Who am I to come along and destroy her home.'

The spider vacated her web for her regular food field recce shortly after Alex had departed. Jayne opened the jar and broke the web scrapping the delicate strands into the jar as she had done regularly since the spider's arrival. She made use of the silken strands in casting her own web. Later she would take great pleasure in watching as the spider returned to her favourite spot and start the long and intricate process of her craft all over again. Catface watched on and purred.

Jayne looked at the gargoyle and the few odd pieces of broken horn. He was a fine specimen. Usually she preferred to work on her kitchen table but she didn't want him inside her house so she had opened the box and settled to work on the garden patio table. Mixing some concrete filler she needed some tools. They were inside. She may also use the bathroom too, now she was up. Noticing the hard skin foot filer she had an idea. She flushed, washed her hands and took the foot filings with her.

She emptied her powdered dead skin into the filler

mix stirring whilst stating her intentions aloud.
Adding her personal message to the mix she started
to fix the horns back into place. It didn't take long. It
was an easy job compared to what she usually did.

'Doddle!' she said standing back to admire her
work, 'Now you just have to wait for him to come for
you.' She spoke to the gargoyle as she spoke to
herself.

Noticing the draining hole through the mouth, she
used the last of the mixture and, pushing it high and
hidden in the aperture, sealed it securely.

Alex picked up the mended gargoyle from Jayne's
garden where she had left it for him as arranged. He
studied it. She had done a skilful job. It was almost as
good as new he could barely see the cracks. She had
advised that, if it were to be displayed in the garden
they should apply some yogurt to it and the elements
would work with it to bring about that discoloured
weathered look, complete with moss. Looking around
he drank in the smell of the garden. It wasn't the
usual subtle floral tones of a cottage garden, rather
more heady, with strong antiseptic whiffs and an
almost sedative quality. He didn't recognize the smells
or the plants, apart from the mint and was that
catnip? On closer inspection it was a well stocked and
all encompassing herb garden.

Taking the gargoyle home he decided not to tell
Mia who had fixed it; no point in causing unnecessary
trouble. She decided that she wanted to hang it on the
wall just outside facing the patio windows. It was
heavy and he checked the solid wall to make sure it
could handle the extra weight. Deciding it could, he

laid the head on the ground and went to find his tools. He brought some yogurt from the fridge too. Drilling into the wall he hung the head. He found it creepy with its horns and the empty concrete grey eyes bore into him and seemed to follow him. It gave him the creeps. Taking a piece of old rag he wiped some yogurt across the form apologizing with a loud 'sorry fella' as the milky white liquid got into the recessed pools of the eyes.

22

The sound of children filled the house. Today was Grace's fourth birthday. Mia could hardly hear herself think as she wondered where those years had gone. Her thoughts were interrupted by a young boy sporting a wizard cape and brandishing a wand as he zoomed by chasing a little girl who was wearing fairy wings.

'Abara...cad...ab...ara! Make Jessie a frog!' he had trouble saying the magic word, which had an immediate effect on the little girl who, now crying, ran along to her mother.

'I don't want to be a frog,' she cried.

'Don't be unkind to your sister Nathan,' their mother caught Mia's eye and mouthed the words, 'Little toad.'

Mia smiled. Time for the cake. She headed back to the kitchen where the large patio doors opened on to the garden. It was a beautiful day and Mia caught the sounds of birds singing, enjoying a momentary respite from the party madness. Turning back to the birthday cake she carefully lit the four pink candy striped candles. She made her way back to the party with the cake carefully dodging the little people.

'Time for the cake!' she raised her voice attempting to be heard.

Her mother, ever the reliable grandmother, appeared right on cue.

'Children come on. It's time for the cake,' Pearl called out to the children closely followed by a louder shout across to her husband, 'Come on Grandad where's the camera? We need an action shot.'

Herb was wearing the camera on a red and black stripy thick strap around his neck. His wife had brought the strap for him. That way the camera would always be to hand on occasions such as this. He had wanted the understated black strap but that was out of stock. Not wanting to wait they had taken the stripy one. Pearl had said it gave him an added artistic flair. He had wondered at the time if it would add flair to his photos.

'Where's Daddy?' asked Grace.

Mia looked across to Pearl, 'Oh hold on. Hold on children,' Pearl said and then asked Herb, 'Go and look for Alex would you love, tell him Grace is ready to blow out her candles.'

Nodding, Herb walked towards the kitchen and out into the garden through the open patio doors. Alex was sitting on the children's swing, looking thoughtful and smoking a cigarette.

'Come on son, Grace is ready to blow out her candles. She is looking for you'.

'Ok.' Alex took a final drag.

'Come on now, Alex, everyone is waiting.'

Alex flicked out his cigarette and following his father-in-law, the two men walked back into the house.

'One, two, three,' Mia smiled across to Alex, starting to sing, 'Happy birthday to you…' she was grateful when everyone started to sing along with her, 'Happy birthday dear Gracie…happy birthday to you!'

Grace was beaming, her little face now illuminated by the candles on the cake. Mia felt a surge of love for her daughter and a sense of relief that the party was going so well. She looked up just as Jayne entered carrying a gift wrapped in a huge silky pink bow. The verse came to an end and was followed by 'three cheers for Grace' which Jayne immediately instigated in a loud excited voice. Mia looked across to Alex, her anger beginning to rage. She needed to get out of the room before she exploded. Alex's eyes moved across to Jayne's. They were standing side by side, Ben and Grace beside them as Herb, blissfully unaware, kept snapping the shutter. Digital cameras were great, no 24 or 36 exposures to restrict him now.

'Oh I forgot the cake slice,' said Mia clocking them and making her excuse with a hasty exit to the kitchen. She was closely followed by Alex, who closed the kitchen door behind them.

'That woman has some nerve!' said Mia, opening and banging closed drawers in her fruitless search for the cake slice.

The sun was coming through the patio door and reflecting on the hanging, large shiny silver witchball. In the slight breeze the movement caused light shapes to dance around the kitchen.

'Calm down Mia!'

'Calm down! How fucking dare you tell me to calm down!'

Back in the party room faint sounds of the

argument were heard over the relative quiet as the children waited for their eagerly anticipated slice of the sweet pink cake. The sounds of nursery rhymes filled the air as Herb quickly turned up the music in an attempt to cover the noise. Grace was transfixed to see Jayne, who was still holding the very pink parcel for her.

'Blow out your candles Grace. Let's make a wish.'

'I hate that bitch!' screamed Mia walking across to the patio doors she noticed the bright shiny witchball illuminated now as the orange sun was just starting to set on the day. Just at that moment, Grace blew out her candles with the delicate puff of a little girl. Anticipating this, Jayne had positioned herself to make her supporting blow. The candles extinguished easily followed by a wisp of grey then black smoke.

Herb looked on wondering why this woman had taken it upon herself to organize blowing the candles. *Too late now, I didn't see that coming.* Falling back on his old faithful party trick, he started showing the kids his finger. He had lost the top of his index finger years ago in an accident at work. Now, by using his full size index finger and thumb of his other hand, with careful bending he made it look like he could make his finger disappear with magic. Nathan, the little wizard boy was wide-eyed with admiration as Jessie screamed. Herb balked at their mother's disapproving look. *Some people just didn't have a sense of humour.*

Back in the kitchen, Mia collapsed under the witchball. On the floor, Alex panicked desperately trying to bring her around when the door opened. Pearl walked in holding the elusive cake slice.

'It was on the table…Alex,' she said spotting her daughter on the floor, 'Mia! What's happened!'

'Call an ambulance! I thought she had fainted but I can't bring her around. Pearl! Pearl! Call an ambulance Pearl!'

23

Florence Renata Bridgestock meditated regularly; sometimes at home, sometimes in the privacy of the back of the shop, if the mood took her. She was one of the first to open herself up to this kind of astral travel long before it became trendy and mainstream. It had been second nature to her ever since she could remember. Not something she had been taught. It was anathema to her when, in her later years, she had seen that people could go on courses to learn how. She found this strange as to her it had always been a natural thing. Only when she was much older could she consider that people could, maybe, be taught the art. Just like Peter and his evasive computer courses.

She stood by her belief that some people have predispositions to certain things. Some were good with computers just as some had green fingers. Life had taught her that only when people had this predisposition could they excel. The correct disposition coupled with passion and energy and they could fly. Nothing was out of the question or impossible.

The overwhelming urge to get her life in order had descended about two days ago. It was making her thoughtful; springing up geysers of thought in her mind she had assumed had long since run dry.

She thought about her decision not to have children. She felt it had been the right one. At her age it would be pointless to think otherwise, still she felt comfort that she had not lived to regret the decision. Peter had in some way filled the void of not having her own son, whilst at the same time reminding her of the pitfalls she had avoided by her abstinence.

In her younger adult years she found the world a harsh place. Well maybe not the world itself. She saw impossible beauty all around her everyday. Beauty which existed at the mercy of mankind and all its shortcomings. She had retreated into her shell in her late thirties opting out of the madness, preferring to keep herself to herself. Her time alone had served to fine tune her third eye which had been there forever. She had lived her life more and more as an observer. It had happened slowly over time and, after initial intermittent bouts of loneliness, she had finally decided that she preferred it and accepted that was the hand that life had served her. She would play it with integrity, even in times of adversity.

Occasionally other people, generally men, had bounded into her life, shattering the peace as destructive as a stray ball shattering glass with its uninvited and intrusive impact. She had almost married once. She exhaled loudly at the thought. Again not with regret but with a satisfied sense of relief. What a lucky escape.

She knew instinctively that her end was in sight.

She was not frightened of death. She knew that there was something else for she had seen it with her own eyes. That was one regret. She missed her eyes. Her seeing eyes. Although with the loss of her physical sight she had found her other senses had soared. She relied heavily on her memories to colour the blackness that was her world now.

Peter came out back to find her sitting there in silence. He was well used to her behaviour. She was often not there even when physically she appeared to be. Respecting her silence he retreated back to the shop front. She called him to let him know that he was not disturbing her work.

'I thought you were busy Aunt. Are you hungry shall I fix you some lunch?' he offered.

'Are you hungry Peter? You really should start looking after yourself. Make sure you eat something, not just look after me.'

'You worry too much. And that is my job to look after you,' he thought for a moment, 'as a matter of fact I am rather peckish.'

'I know I heard your stomach rumbling in the shop.'

'Well there is nothing wrong with your hearing then is there? You could hear a pin drop in Penzance!'

She smiled. 'So what delights are on the menu today?' her enquiry was tinged with a sprinkle of sarcasm, for Peter was a man of very simple tastes and nothing illustrated this more than his diet, 'Crab and rocket salad? Calamari rings with avocado?' *Such a waste having such a bland diet what with us living on top of the seaside*.

'Cheese sandwich do you?' ignoring her humour which was not lost on him.

'I'll have some pickle on mine son.'

Her use of the term son stalled him. She wondered for a second too where that had come from. They both recognized that she had never called him that before.

'As you wish dear Aunt,' he could not think of anything else to say that would let her know that he had heard and appreciated this term of endearment. His inclusion of the word dear seemed to him inadequate but to call her anything else was so unnatural and not him. He could think of nothing else he could have said, even when later her words played again on a loop in his head. Her calling him 'son' had meant a great deal and had validated her feelings to him. He knew that he was difficult to show affection to he thought as he spread the pickle on her bread. He picked out the lumps which he knew she hated. Occasionally, when they had unimportant words he had, to his shame, left them in a pathetic act of defiance. He closed the sandwich and took the knife cutting it carefully and thoughtfully into four. In that moment it occurred to him that she would not always be there. She was clearly having a thoughtful day too. He took her sandwich.

'Did you remember the pickle?' she caught a whiff of it as she spoke, 'Thank you Peter. I hope you left out the lumps today. They play havoc with my plate.'

He was silently grinning.

'Laugh out loud Peter. It is good for you. Think I don't know your game eh?' she took a bite and chewed before continuing, 'You'll explode like a big pent up volcano one day.'

He didn't take her up on her offer instead suppressing the laugh in his belly. It made his flat and empty stomach jiggle up and down. He took his lunch back to the counter where he ate his half a sandwich; no butter, no pickle just cheese in a slice of bread, uncut just folded over.

'You should taste life's pickle Peter! she called from behind the curtain, 'You might just find you like it.'

He ignored her. He knew what he liked.

Today, as always, he opened and dealt with the post on account of his aunt's blindness. She insisted on him reading all correspondence to her. He bent down to pick up the pile of letters on the shop mat. Lunch over, he turned the closed sign in the window to open and went back to the counter to deal with the mail. Most of the envelopes were brown, bills and invoices from suppliers.

There was one handwritten in an unfamiliar hand. The letters were large, flowing with flicks and flourishes at the end of their formations, in purple ink. He opened Mia's thank you letter just as his aunt called out her daily enquiry 'Is there any post?' He made them both tea and settled down to go through the brown letters before reading Mia's letter aloud to his aunt.

'I knew she was the right person to have it,' she said sensing her nephew's disapproval.

Hearing the tinkle signaling a customer he went out front leaving his aunt holding the letter. She knew that it was important to get the witchball in safe hands. She wasn't getting any younger. She had no children of her own to pass it on to. Peter was her only family now and he didn't believe in the power. She felt no guilt in giving it away to Mia. It was too powerful to fall into the wrong hands. She had been on the look out for quite some time for a successor. Mia was not the first customer to enquire after the ball. Big bucks had been offered by an American just a couple of weeks ago. In spite of his assurances that it would be kept in his family, Florence had known that he would be selling it on, along with its witchy English history, for a vast profit to some poor, probably unsuspecting customer. She knew that Mia was different. Mia. She knew her name now too. She sensed that the young woman was one of those rare finds, in her own way as precious as the witchball, that couldn't be bought with money. She also sensed from her aura that she was an emotional power station and the witchball would serve her well as an aid to her protection. The letter of thanks she now held was a welcome validation that she had indeed made the right choice of the witchball's new charge.

She had spent the past few days putting her house in order, mostly with the help of Peter. He was a good boy really. Just not in the least bit 'open' to anything that wasn't scientifically proven. Rigid as a stone and set in his ways, dismissive of anything he didn't understand as coincidence or folly. She wished he would find a partner. He had never married. She couldn't even remember him having had a girlfriend. Never even known him to have shown an interest in a pretty girl. She had asked him what Mia looked like. He had said, and she believed him, that he couldn't remember. He wasn't one of those homosexuals though. The thought never crossed her mind although she did ask him what that fella with her was like, just to be sure. He had responded with a dismissive, 'ignorant Londoner' not even gracing her question with an answer. She knew he was way off the mark there. He had not picked up on Perry's sexual persuasion either. No. He was not a good judge of character. He'd had a very sheltered upbringing. She had known him all his life. He had been a loner as boy and man. She had tried to cuddle him only once. When her sister, his mother, had passed away. She had tried to hug him but he had backed off with a visible wince. She had let go terrified that he would break and disintegrate like a rotten, dried out piece of old wood. She decided never to try again. He had not been around enough people to make an informed decision about people's characters at all. His energy ran low and slow. Nothing for any afterlife to tap into, highjack maybe but she suspected his light shone too flat and dark for him to be of any real interest to them. She doubted the absence of the witchball would have any real consequence to his life at all. Although she knew that when the shop shut down soon, not helped by slow trade and the recent recession, he would pounce on the fact that its demise had all been a consequence of the witchball being given away to those 'uncouth and ignorant Londoners'.

Florence had not thought anymore about the ball. She was looking forward to absolute retirement. She had thought about closing the shop for a while but she was concerned for Peter's wellbeing. With little else in his life but work she wondered what he would do with his time. Money had continued to come into the shop but had definitely been affected by the onslaught of this internet invention. It was a concept unnatural to her, she liked to 'see' and feel things before she bought. Peter had tried to keep up but he was not au fait with technology so although he occasionally bought bargains online, sales were strictly from the shop. Knowing that the shop was on borrowed time, she tried again to broach the subject one afternoon when the shop was even more quiet than usual. The little bell had failed to tinkle all day. It was raining outside. Dismal day equaled dismal sales.

'I think you should start to think of something else to do Peter dear.'

'What do you mean Aunt?'

'We can't keep the shop going like this for much longer. It's no use burying your head in the sand. There is more going out than coming in. I can't keep subsidizing this place. Something has to change. Far better to take the bull by the horns, Peter.'

'Sell the shop? But what else would I do?'

'Put your thinking cap on. Change is coming. It is always best to be prepared not just have change thrust upon you.'

'Is there something you are not telling me Aunt? Have you put the shop up for sale?'

'No but I think you should set the ball rolling. As soon as you can.'

'That's it. It's the ball. We have been here for all these years and as soon as you let the witchball go things go downhill.'

'What drivel!' his response was so predictable, 'You do the books, you do the maths. This has been coming for months, years even. I want to enjoy the little time I have left. Not be struggling and throwing good money after bad.'

'The math,' he corrected her 'I'll try the web again. I'll go on a course. I can learn.'

'You could have done that before.'

'I know but it's not too late now is it?'

'It would be a way to keep the business going without the shop overheads.'

'But we have always had the shop. It's been in our family forever. We can't give up now.'

'We can't keep going either. Not unless you want to run us both into the ground. Now, look into your night school. If you are sure that's what you want but call the estate agents or I shall. It's up to you.'

Peter huffed knowing he had no choice but to act on his aunt's instructions. She had been good to him over the years and he knew deep down that she was right. There was no denying that business had been on a downturn for a long while now. How he hated change. It scared him. What would he do next? How would he fill his days? He knew that the college idea was just a pipe dream. The thought of being in a room full of strangers filled him with dread. Still he had to do something. At least working in the shop he had felt like he was in some way paying his way. It was never meant to be a permanent thing. He had stayed on with his aunt after his mother's funeral and it just sort of went on from there. Then, when his aunt's eyesight has failed completely, he had stayed on. It was an easy decision. He liked Cornwall. It was quiet and it suited him. He looked back across the years wondering where they had gone.

'Regrets are futile,' said his aunt, 'You have lots of life ahead of you Peter. Look forward now, not back. In another thirty years' time you want to be looking back with a smile. This is the first step now. Make sure you live wise. Nothing you do leaves you. Everything comes back. Good and bad. There's no escape, you reap what you sow. You won't get another chance.'

He knew she was talking sense but he hated to hear it. She always had a way of being able to look inside his soul. She was doing the same now and he felt like a child again. He made his excuses and went out front to the shop. Anything to get away from her and her blasted wisdom.

'In another thirty years you'll be out of time. Like I am, now.' She spoke under her breath, more to herself this time than to him.

24

The familiar stars whirled bright before Mia's eyes. She knew this feeling. It was peaceful and comforting. There were no colours this time, she noticed. She couldn't remember settling down to meditate either. With practice had she now progressed so far that she could cut right through the rainbow spectrum? As she watched the many shooting stars cease, she had found herself surrounded by blackness. She could hear the faraway sound of hollow screams. She thought she recognized the voice. It sounded like her mother though she had never before heard her shout 'Mia' in such a high pitched way. *Was that panic in her voice?* Her mum was calling for her. She needed her. Something was wrong.

Mia urged herself to go back. She willed her mind to reconnect with her body. This had too become automatic with practice. Only this time nothing was happening. This blackness was unfamiliar. There was silence now. She opened her eyes. With the same anticipation of waking in the dead of night she waited for her eyes to readjust and focus to the darkness. She heard a distorted gravelly voice. It had a kind of underwater quality. The words boomed and then fell away like the sound equivalent of a camera coming into focus. Finally, the sounds became sharp as the hideous, bellowing, twisted voice spoke with clarity 'we are watching you!'

Mia's ears pricked and her eyes strained in the darkness. Looking above her then left and then right; nothing but blackness, pitch blackness. She looked below her. She registered colour. *What colour?* Silver. Glinting. Peering closer, the shiny silver colour took on a transparency. She reached out to touch the shiny area beneath her weightless self. The familiar feeling of her lifeless limb moving was not as scary as it had been that time in bed. She had trained herself not to panic. She had trained herself to return. Only this time she felt blocked. She couldn't get back.

Forcing her lifeless arm, with the weightlessness of an astronaut, she traced the curvature of the silver space beneath her. For a second she thought she was looking into a mirror as she saw herself below. Then she saw Alex and her mother. She watched on as Alex bent over her lifeless body. Looking 360 degrees around her she saw the silver outline of the arc encasing her. She was trapped. As it slowly dawned on her where she was her horrified silent scream was given another voice. The sound of her mother's blood curdling howl.

Perry phoned Mia's home letting it ring out. There was no answer. The mobile went direct to answerphone. He hung up without leaving a message.

He was becoming convinced that Mia was the source of his recent discomfort; he was having real trouble settling down to anything. He thought about driving there again. No. He would wait a little longer. He was sure that he had Mia's parents' telephone number somewhere. He would do something useful and look through his old address books still filled with old numbers, long since called and long before mobiles and computers. All was not well he knew that already from his recent malaise, the ringing out phones merely seemed to confirm it. He hated not knowing what was wrong and his imagination went into overdrive. He needed to ground himself and take back control. So he decided looking through the books could wait. He would go for a long walk first.

Mia stirred. She was vaguely aware of some time having passed. There was no sign of the silver edging to the still darkness now. All was silent. She rose to her ethereal feet. Unsure of where she was going or what she should do now, she glided along with the lightness of a summer moth. She enjoyed the feeling of weightlessness. Going back to her body always felt like home but it also felt enclosed and restricted. It felt just like those gloomy dismal winter days when you are at home and can't open the windows because it's icy cold outside. Before the warm weather arrives and you can finally throw open all the windows and stir up the air and lift that heavy stale trapped feeling. The skin and bone gown was cumbersome and heavy. Only now when she couldn't reach it was she missing it. Feeling vulnerable and exposed, she kept on in the dark.

Her brain continued to give her body the signal to walk, only it directed phantom limbs. *Maybe this is what it feels like when you lose a body part?* She remembered her dad had said as much when he lost the top of his finger. He said that he had felt it for some time after and that his brain had to learn that it was no longer there. In any case she knew now, without doubt, that this was definitely what it felt like to lose a body.

Yet her mind was still fully aware. In the darkness she came across a white corridor. The rows of white doors lined up one after the other, uniform and indistinct. Each bearing the number 70, they stretched out before her in a seemingly never ending maze. Her consciousness suggested that she may be lucid dreaming. She would wake up soon, get dressed, be with the kids, have a normal day. *Was it a normal day?* Something told her it wasn't just any ordinary day. Something was showing her music, balloons, a pretty pink cake. It was Grace's birthday party. The fleeting memory was distant and elusive.

The urge to open one of the doors overwhelmed her. The only thing stopping her was the fear of what she might find on the other side. The dilemma played itself out in her head. She wondered was the owner of the bellowing voice watching her now? She continued moving along the corridor wondering how she would choose which door to open, should that urge win. They all looked the same. White. The digits 70 were large and silver. Studying them closely she instinctively reached out for a handle. There wasn't one but the slight enquiring brushing of her hand against the whiteness had made her decision. In an instant she found herself standing inside the whiteness of the room. Then she saw her.

She studied her long tasseled tresses. They were matted and knotted. The dull auburn mass was the only thing distinguishing her from the walls. Encased in white she appeared to have no arms. Mia quickly realized her body was swaddled in a white straightjacket, her arms present but useless, tied tightly behind her back as they were. Looking into those lifeless eyes, they were looking intently back at her. They were without warmth, smudged with heavy black circles. They were tired. Without hope. No sooner had she accepted that she was looking at herself, the blackness enveloped her again.

The acrid smell of the hospital ward invaded Alex's nostrils bringing with it memories long since buried that he would much rather forget. He walked along the white corridors. Somebody had carefully arranged art for sale on the wall, probably in an attempt to cheer the place up. Instead it just served to highlight, as if there could be any doubt, that he was in a hospital. He had been for a cigarette, the need to escape overwhelming, as the smell and memories had flooded him with panic. His footsteps echoed along the outstretched maze. Now as he searched his way back he was lost. It all looked the same.

He swallowed the feeling of panic as it started to rise again. He spotted the large canvas with the foot high quirky purple shoes. It hung like a beacon, its glitter twinkling and sparkling, outside Mia's ward guiding him in the right direction, back to her. He made a mental note to buy it for her. It was definitely her kind of thing, although not his, yet at this moment he loved it as it served as a landmark to where she now lay.

Herb came through the door. 'The doctors can't tell us anything. We just have to wait. I am going to phone Pearl, she'll be worried. She was going to see if she could get someone to watch the kids and then she'll be here.'

Just then they spotted her coming towards them, her frantic face ashen white. Herb hugged her as she broke down, firing broken fragments of questions through her tears. Herb could only repeat what he had told Alex. There was no news, the doctors were doing all they could but yes she was still alive. Saying those words aloud opened the floodgates and the three of them cried together. A passing nurse showed them a family waiting room but left briskly after assurances that Mia was in the best place and that someone would be back with news, as soon as there was any. They sat in silence.

'Are the kids ok, what did you tell them?' Alex finally spoke.

'They are fine. I told them Mummy is not feeling very well. Everyone left the party pretty quickly. The woman with the pink present, Jayne is it, offered to stay and watch the kids. She insisted. Said that she had watched them before,' said Pearl seeking assurances from Alex that she had done the right thing, her loyalties having been stretched between wanting to be there for both her daughter and her grandchildren. Seeing this and the sadness in her eyes, Alex decided it would be best to say nothing.

'Mia will be fine,' he squeezed her hand in an empty gesture of reassurance that he didn't know whether even he himself believed. His eyes met Herb's.

'Of course she will.' As Herb, sat on the other side of her, spoke the words his eyes looked down.

Mia felt alone in the darkness. The whiteness of the corridor had long since gone although the vision had not left her. Should she stay still or keep wandering? The silence kept being broken by the occasional disturbing sound of faraway whines. She counted her blessings that she had not heard the threatening voice again that had spoken of watching her, though the gripping fear it had instilled was also difficult to shake off. Should she stay put and see what happens?

She stayed still and tried to block out the fear and the faraway echoes, willing herself to wake up. It was impossible and the distant cries seemed to be getting closer, although she herself had not moved an inch. She felt her senses heighten, her sense of fear overtaking her as she tried to work out how to protect herself, when she couldn't see what hidden dangers the blackness might hold. The wailing cries were getting louder and she strained, trying to assess from which direction they were coming from within the darkness. Only they seemed to be all around her, suffocating her, from every direction.

25

A doctor had come and gone. Mia was in a coma that was all he could tell them at this point. They should go home and rest. They would be informed of any changes in her condition immediately. They had quickly agreed that Mia should not be left alone with at least one of them there at all times. It was agreed that Alex should go home first and call around friends for help and support to look after the kids. As he drove home he went through a mental list of friends he might call. Well, primarily, a list of Mia's friends. Under the circumstances it was plain wrong that Jayne was looking after them now. Mia would be livid. Thinking back to the incident with Jayne his face burned with shame. He dismissed the thought quickly. Now was the time to be constructive.

The names that popped forward were limited since, by her own admission, Mia had let some of her closer friendships go when they moved away. It would be a tough call now to telephone out of the blue and expect people to change their own routines to help. Besides, most people just lived too far away to be in a position to be there. He decided that he should find Mia's address book and let people know and see if anyone came forward with offers of help. Social networking would have made his task easier but Mia had considered this so impersonal, not to mention a threat to her privacy and refused to get on the bandwagon, certain that in time others would soon come to the same conclusion.

He would phone Carol and Perry first. He was certain that Carol would be there in an instant. He pulled over and found the number straight away, listed in Mia's mobile. It went straight to answerphone. She was away working in Paris. *Merd*. He decided against leaving a message, pointless panicking her. He would call again and explain in person. He needed to let Perry know too. Another answerphone. Technology was great until you really needed to talk to someone urgently. Knowing that Perry fielded all of his calls and rarely answered the phone, he was going to leave a quick message. He wouldn't go into detail. He'd intended to say that he would explain when they spoke but the words stuck in his throat and he couldn't speak. Instead he quickly hung up deciding that he would do it later.

Back inside the house was quiet. The smell of cooking filled the air. Alex's stomach gurgled in appreciation and his mouth watered. He remembered that he hadn't eaten anything since yesterday's party sausage rolls. Jayne was waiting in the dining room, the table fully laid complete with lit candles. All traces of the party, gone.

'Hello Alex I thought you may be hungry.'

'Where are the kids?' Alex ignored his stomach

pangs.

'Tucked up in bed. Good as gold. Drink?'

He didn't answer as he made his way back out of the room and up the stairs to check on his sleeping children. Grace was sleeping soundly. Ben was snuggled in his cot sound asleep too. He would get rid of Jayne and then have a shower and get some shut eye himself. Tomorrow he would call around Mia's friends first thing. Pearl had agreed to collect the kids and take them during the day so he could go back to the hospital. She would go back to the hospital in the evening. They would manage in shifts until they could find someone else to help. Anyway the kids could go back to their usual routines next week. He would have to get back to work at some point though he couldn't even think about that now. Hopefully Mia would be back on her feet anytime soon; he couldn't allow himself to think anything else. In the meantime it was important to maintain some normality to the kids' routine. Back in the dining room, Jayne had dished up two meals.

'How did you know I was coming back?'

'We all have to eat,' she shrugged, her answer effortlessly evasive.

He felt awkward sitting down to eat with this woman whilst his wife was laying unconscious back at the hospital. She had made the food and although he wanted to get her out of there as soon as possible, he felt he should be grateful and his manners and stomach won over.

'Thank you for all you have done Jayne. You should get off home after this, we'll cope from here.' He sat down and started to eat, savouring every mouthful, the taste of the food intensified by the short term famine of the past twenty four hours. The warmth of the food was comforting and he felt the stress of Mia's collapse temporarily lifting. They ate in silence. His eyes were heavy. He was full up. Contented and tired. He needed to sleep. The urge was suddenly overwhelming.

The quilt tight around his neck, Alex was slumbering in that magical place between sleep and awake. Stirring, he heard the sound of footsteps on the wooden bedroom floor. Listening, the footsteps were fast and much heavier than a child's, the pattering, tap-tap, tap-tap rhythm was also not of the kind made by two legs. It sounded like a dog was circling the bed and he felt it's two front paws lunge.

'Daddy!' said Grace jumping on him, waking him completely.

He pulled the quilt around her as she snuggled up next to him.

'Where's Mummy?'

It took a few seconds for him to remember. He couldn't even remember getting to bed last night. Mia was in hospital. The events of the past couple of days came flooding back.

'Ten minutes Grace,' he said snuggling up to his daughter, 'Then we have to get up, Nanny is coming over. Mummy is with the doctors you'll be able to see her when she is feeling a bit better.'

He was surprised to see Jayne still there when they went down for breakfast.

'Morning Alex. Morning Grace.'

'I thought you left last night?'

'You zonked out, you were in no fit state to look

after them,' putting bread in the toaster.

'Well I am here now. Thank you Jayne but really, we have taken up enough of your time. You should go,' looking at his watch, Pearl was due soon. It would look pretty weird her showing up to find them looking like they were playing happy families.

'You are welcome, I am happy to help and besides, I have nothing else to do. I'll just have a coffee and get Ben up and ready.'

'Ben never sleeps this late. Did he have a bad night? Lucky you stayed, I must've slept right through his crying.'

'No he slept straight through.'

Alex poured milk on Grace's cereal and ate his toast.

26

Mia held her breath; the noise was circling her now. The wailing had been replaced by a sort of low shallow breathing which seemed to have invaded her head.

Opening her eyes slowly to the darkness still surrounding her she searched, trying to find the chink, that slightest scratch in the silver now spinning around her. She moved closer to the shining outline of the space but, again and again, it became transparent, before growing in front of her eyes into an arc again. As the spinning ceased, the darkness was gradually replaced on one side and below her with silver light giving her the impression she was sitting on a crescent shaped moon.

She could see her kitchen! There was Alex sitting at the table. And there was little Grace. They were eating breakfast. She shifted suddenly fearing the blackness more, that she may somehow fall off its precipice to be lost in the darkness forever.

She pushed her face as close as she could to get

the best view of her husband and daughter. She thought she heard barking, loud, menacing barking. Concentrating on the slit of light, her eyes were suddenly met with wide, hungry looking eyes as black as coal and fangs dripping with saliva. The wolf's growling filled her being as she fell back in sheer horror.

She took a few seconds to compose herself. She had recognized the wolf immediately as the dog that she had seen Grace with on the stairs. The same one that she had caught a glimpse of in the park?

Grace watched on as her dog growled up at the witchball. Looking across at her daddy, she knew he was totally unaware of its presence, as he chomped on his toast and read the newspaper.

Jayne came in carrying Ben. Her one look at the dog was enough to stop its noise as it came to heel.

'Grace go along and get your little overnight bag we packed last night.'

Grace did as she was told heading to her bedroom followed, without instruction, by her canine companion.

'Shit!' said Alex, spilling coffee on his tie, 'Hold on Grace I will come and help you find it.'

Jayne put Ben down on the floor with some toys whilst she rinsed through the breakfast dishes. Ben, being at the age when he wanted to start exploring, had started crawling and headed over towards the patio windows. He liked to watch the birds that ate from the bird table there. He moved with the unsteady wobbling of a just starting out crawler. His balance was challenged by a wooden toy brick and he tumbled over, landing upside down on his back. Looking up he was mesmerized by the large silver shiny witchball.

Mia had mustered her courage to look again, certain that, if she couldn't break through the silver vortex, that malicious mutt couldn't either. She gingerly peered out again. Ben was lying on his back looking up at her and giggling. The sight of her baby made her catch her breath. He looked ok, happy enough, he wasn't crying. She wondered could he see her too? Gurgling he picked up the red brick and put it in his mouth. It was too large and heavy for his little hands and he dropped it again.

'Mmm,' the word was tentative but clear.

He had seen her!

Mia watched as he was scooped up and taken away. Not by Alex. It was a woman's frame. She had not seen the face but she would know her anywhere. Anger bubbled in her at the realization that it was Jayne. She willed her to look up but Jayne kept her eyes well averted from the witchball; just being near it made her blood run cold and her very spirit cower and contract.

'Grace,' called Jayne, 'Come along, have you found the bag?' taking Ben she headed up the stairs to see what was keeping Grace.

She passed Grace coming out of her room, bag in hand. The door bell rang.

'That'll be Nanny let's go and let her in,' said Alex, tucking down his fresh tie and taking Grace by the hand.

As Alex opened the door to Pearl, Jayne was coming down the stairs carrying Ben.

Pearl looked puzzled but said nothing as she hugged Grace and followed them into the kitchen.

'I have packed my bag Nanny. And I have Ben's

bag all ready too. Jayne helped me. Mummy is not well she is in the hospital with the doctors they are going to make her better'.

Mia's ears pricked up. She wasn't in the hospital she wanted to scream at them. *I am here!*

Jayne came into the room and offered Ben, who was excited to see his nanny, to Pearl.

'Jayne you have been very kind,' she said kissing her grandson hello, 'but you must have things to do now. We can manage from here thank you.'

'Nonsense Pearl.'

They had never been formally introduced and Pearl was slightly taken aback by Jayne's familiarity. There was something about the woman that she didn't take to. Why was she so keen to help anyway? Mia had barely mentioned her. If they had been close she was sure that her daughter would have mentioned her before. She couldn't even recall her speaking of any new friends even in passing. It wasn't like Mia to make friends easily. She never had, preferring the history she shared with old friends. Friends that she knew well, and that in turn, knew her well.

Jayne sensed that Pearl was trying to work her out and how she fitted into Mia's new life.

'Alex has been very kind to me. My car was stuck. I was very grateful and am happy to help now.' She wondered if this would be enough to settle Pearl's enquiring mind.

Mia listened in.

'That's Alex all over. Anything to help anyone out,' said Pearl.

'That's what I have been telling her Pearl. It was nothing.'

'Nothing to you. But it meant a lot to me. A

damsel in distress!'

That was it thought Pearl taking Grace to her room to get some more toys. Jayne, without invitation, followed. She played the woman in distress card, flattering a man to worm her way in and play to his ego. Women like her were everywhere.

'You don't need to make such a big thing of it, he would've done it for anyone love, even a hulking great mountain of a man!' Pearl spoke with a jokey lilt to her voice knowing this player of a woman would still pick up and hopefully heed her disapproval. Come to think of it Mia had mentioned her, just not by name. Wasn't she the one that had come around unannounced laden with homemade biscuits and jam?

Herb was bored sitting around waiting for Pearl to get the kids' stuff together. Ben was playing on the kitchen floor by the patio doors so he started to flick through his digital camera, whizzing through the pictures that he'd already seen. He must get around to downloading them; he was as usual putting it off. He looked around the kitchen. *Was there time to make a cup of tea?* Pearl had said that she would only be five minutes; yeah right, he knew her five minutes. He didn't even want any more tea; he'd been drinking so much of it lately, mostly the pissy weak vending machine variety.

Standing up, he paced around for a bit; walking to the door he looked up the stairs listening for any signs that his wife and granddaughter were making a move. Nothing. He dismissed the thought to call up and chivvy them along. Camera still in hand, instead he took a few random shots. The pink and purple orchid on the telephone table and then the chandelier; first with the light on, then with it off, he zoomed in and out. Catching sight of himself in the gold gilt-framed hall mirror, he took a shot of himself. God he looked old. *Better get back to Ben.*

He was still in the same position, beneath that big silver bauble, he seemed fascinated by it. *Mmm now that would make an arty shot.* If he could get the angle right, maybe he could capture the baby's reflection in it too. He clicked away, repositioning his stance from several angles. Ben obliged, smiling and gurgling. A couple of times Herb thought he heard him attempt to say Mummy and point his little finger in the air.

Suddenly, overcome by a great surge of love, he grabbed his grandson lifting him into a hug. *This whole bloody episode was so unfair!* Hearing the girls coming down the stairs, he fought to regain his composure; they mustn't see him lose it, they needed him to be strong. His mobile phone rang. It was the doctor they were needed at the hospital.

'You go to the hospital, Mia needs you,' said Jayne, 'The kids will be fine here with me'.

The doctor had said that Mia was showing signs of distress. They left for the hospital straight away.

Jayne smiled as she watched the car screech away. She took Grace and Ben back to the kitchen settling them both down on the area below the shiny ball. Giving Ben toys and Grace her colouring pens and pencils she instructed them to play nicely. She was careful not to look directly at the ball, keeping her distance from it. Grace grizzled that she didn't want to do drawing, she wanted her mummy.

Mia could see her children. They were crying for her and it broke her heart that she couldn't go to them. What were Alex and her mother thinking of, leaving her precious children with that wicked witch of a woman? Was she the only one that could see through her? She berated herself for not having confided her fears to her mother when she had the chance. She had done so for good reason. She had not wanted to worry her. Although more than that, she had not wanted to give voice to her worries through fear of sounding like some silly jealous adolescent. She wondered if Alex had told Perry she was in the hospital? She was sure that he would come soon if he knew. Would he overcome his fear of hospitals to see her? She hoped that he wouldn't and that he would come to the house instead. No. There was no reason for him to come to the house when, for all he knew, she was in the hospital. What about Carol, would she come? She remembered back to their last conversation. She was working on some new project in Paris at a big new product launch. She wouldn't expect her to be back in the UK for a while. *How much time had passed?*

Ben fell asleep on the floor; his dummy had fallen from his mouth, discarded now on the carpet beside him. Grace was drawing. Mia could make out the pencil outline of a dog. Grace had carefully coloured its eyes in the blackest black felt-tip. It's teeth were large pointed fangs, large and out of proportion. Mia watched on as she coloured them in crimson red. The subject of her latest creation lay beside her, a willing model, perfectly still but for the rise and fall of his grey fur covered haunches, as he breathed in and out. Jayne laid the table. Mia watched on in disbelief as this friend in disguise prepared *her* food to feed *her* children. Mia lashed out with frustration; her loud scream echoed and ricocheted around her.

'Come on Grace. Sit up the table, lunch is ready,'

said Jayne picking up *her* sleeping Ben and strapping him in his high chair.

'Ok Jayne. Look at my picture. We can put it on the fridge like Mummy says.'

Taking the picture, Jayne looked at the blood red fangs. Not suitable material for a little girl. She screwed the paper up into a ball and threw it in the bin. The look from Jayne was enough to tell Grace not to argue and she sat at the table.

'Do you want juice?' Jayne offered.

'No.'

'What?' barked Jayne.

'No I don't want juice it will make my teeth black.'

'What?' repeated Jayne.

'I don't want black teeth. You showed me.' Grace was slightly scared now.

'No what? What is the magic word little girl?' Jayne's voice took on its gravelly tone.

'No thank you Jayne,' Grace complied, 'May I have a glass of water please?'

'That's more like it. You may.' Jayne poured her a glass of water.

Ben looked on from his high chair now, rubbing his sleepy eyes, dipping his soldiers into his runny boiled egg.

The telephone rang. Jayne listened as Herb told her that Mia was still showing signs that she was distressed. Would she be able to stay and keep looking after the children so they could all be there for Mia? He thanked her when she said that of course she would and she put down the receiver. At least some one in this family was grateful for all that she was doing for them.

'Eat up!' she told Grace.

'I am finished,' said Grace, 'Just got to smash the shells through.'

'What? Stop making a mess now!'

'Mummy says we have to smash through the egg shells so witches can't rest there.'

'Stop it!' Jayne snatched away the egg cups with the egg shells still in tact, 'You silly little girl!' throwing them in the bin.

Someone was at the front door.

'Hello. I need to speak to Mia,' said Mildred from next door in her elocution lesson tones.

'Tough,' Jayne shrugged 'She's not here.'

'Alex?'

'Look lady, I am here. Now what do you want?'

'Where's Mia and Alex?' in the silence the question was left hanging in the air, 'Look I don't want any trouble, is that dog yours?'

'Dog? What dog?'

'You too! What the hell is going on?'

Jayne said nothing in response. She eyeballed the well spoken woman. She must have been about forty five, with perfectly quaffed hair, wearing well cut, shimmy shammy clothes that swayed as she moved. Getting hot under the collar, her actions were becoming increasingly animated. Jayne remained silent watching the red heat rising in the woman; she seemed ready to blow. Jayne watched on, the silence becoming palpable.

Moving rapidly now as if she had ants in her pants, Mildred felt strange. She said nothing more, looking at the old woman before her she wondered if perhaps she were deaf. She looked like an old crone, wrinkled, dressed from head to toe in black, apart from the shocking red flowing hair that would have been more in place on a much younger woman. The dry lines on her face were etched deep and set telling their own twisted sad story without words; these were definitely not laughter lines. She wondered how many times this woman had been wolf whistled, tooted or accosted from behind, to the shock of the poor unsuspecting suitor when she turned her head. *Could she be Alex's mum?* The woman continued staring back at her, making her feel uncomfortable and her face seemed to be ageing by the second. Mildred decided there and then she had to get away and quick; she would come back when Alex or Mia were at home. Watching her hasty retreat, Jayne simply closed the door.

Mia was exhausted with anger and frustration. She had tried again to get back. She knew now that she was in the hospital. She didn't know which one but guessed at King George's as that was the closest by. She had been there before. Only once but she calmed herself and visualized the place hoping that, by knowing where her body was, she would somehow will herself back to it successfully this time. It wasn't working.

It was dark when Alex returned home. Jayne had bathed the kids and put them to bed. She was in the bath herself when she heard Alex come in. She listened as he called out downstairs and then heard him climbing the stairs to check on the kids. She climbed out of the warm scented bubbles and stood facing the open door as she dried herself. Seeing Alex heading towards the bathroom, before he had spotted her, she let her towel drop slightly and feigned surprise when he 'caught' her almost naked, all tits and ginger pussy.

'Cover yourself up!' he said as he walked on by.

Jayne pulled on Mia's silk bathrobe that was hanging there on the hook behind the bathroom door. She followed Alex to the kitchen, where he sat having poured himself a whiskey.

'It's time to leave Jayne.'

'It's late Alex. I'll go tomorrow,' she said helping herself to a drink.

'No. No Jayne you will go tonight. Now.'

Mia heard Alex's raised voice and peeked through the crack in the silver. He was sitting in the dark so there was little to distinguish between the dark of the kitchen and that of the ball. She saw a flash of red silk swirl by. The bitch was wearing her bathrobe! She tried to still her thumping heart, throbbing in her ears. She was incensed and finding it hard to hear. Crouching down she strained her eyes and ears.

'But I've planned a special dinner,' she sat on the edge of the table, letting the bathrobe fall open, 'What are you hungry for Alex?'

'Are you mad woman! My wife is lying in hospital. She is dying!'

Mia flinched.

'Oh come on Alex it's nothing you haven't seen before don't come all innocent now.'

Mia heard the words clearly. She had to get away, couldn't bear to hear what might follow. With her last remaining drop of energy she willed herself to move. She didn't know where to or what would greet her there as she felt her way in the gloom.

'They are telling us we should prepare ourselves to

switch off her life support.'

The words penetrated Mia. They may as well finish the job she thought, the words she had just heard had practically killed her anyway. She felt herself falling away.

27

Away from the silver chink with its window on the familiar routines of her house, Mia had lost all track of time. The infinite blackness held no clues as to the time of day. It seemed that time had no place here. She had tried to move on but it soon became clear that she was just floating around and around in circles. She had stopped unsure of her next move. Sitting now in the dark, she was alone again with her thoughts.

In life she had conditioned herself not to dwell on her thoughts. Her busy life, at first in the event planning office and then the arrival of her children and the new house, had not allowed time for such indulgences. Here she had no such distractions. She thought of her children and missed touching them and their smell. Seeing them like that had given her a welcome assurance that they were ok. She thought of Jayne. How dare that opportunist woman just walk into her life like that. She thought of Alex with feelings of anger stemming from hurt and disappointment that he could have allowed all this to happen.

The feelings of love, hurt, betrayal and many others she had yet to identify, span around in her very core. She heard the sound of echoing laughter. Not the kind that indicated happiness. This was the menacing sound of someone or something enjoying her predicament. Instinctively she knew that her innermost feelings had created a change in vibration. A sort of spiritual body language.

She felt the presence before her, before she saw it. The rainbow colours of the spectrum danced and swirled culminating into intense purples, greens and yellows before taking on an almost holographic appearance of a man. His outline, although clearly masculine was fluid, like a coloured fog, constantly moving. He spoke without words; she heard the voice within her. It was not like the tangible sound of the bellowing voice or the laughter. It told her gently that she was in danger. She should heed her own realization that her feelings would betray her to the dangers that were all around. They knew of her arrival. They had felt and seen her love and tenderness. She shouldn't be here. It was a mistake. It was out of place here and made her an easily identifiable positive energy distinguishable in the sea of dark forces. Besides that, it was not her time.

She felt the kindness within this other entity giving her consciousness the advice. Close down. Here is no place for those feelings. Don't forget they make you an easy target. Just keep going the energy urged her. Without words she offered thanks and an assurance that she had heard his message. She felt inquisitive as to how he had found himself here. As she watched the colours started to spin, gently at first, before rotating into a speeding multi-coloured vortex that disappeared into the returning darkness with a slight swooshing sound. It popped as it disappeared like an old television shutting down transmission.

She had seen clearly what had driven him here. It was awful and she could see how this intrinsically good soul had been tortured and embittered by pain and negativity. She knew she must heed the warning. She would fight the urge to peer once more through the silver chink. She wondered where he was urging her to go. Then it dawned on her that just keep going meant do not give up. She had to get back before any decision was made to terminate her life that was hanging by a thread within that hospital bed and keep moving before whatever was making those vile threatening noises found her.

Perry felt dreadful. He was fielding his calls, not interested in speaking to anyone but Mia. Generally they had a sort of telepathic thing going on; thinking about one another would inevitable be followed shortly after with a call one way or the other. He had been thinking almost solidly about her for the past couple of days. He had dismissed the fleeting idea that perhaps she had gone away on holiday. In this day and age with mobile telecommunications, people still stayed in touch. Something was wrong, he was sure of it.

Feeling ungrounded and fluid, Mia kept moving unsure of where she was heading. The continuing unsettling noises becoming the background soundtrack to her destination unknown journey. She felt she was going around and around in circles. Nothing made any sense any more. She had given up trying to think herself back to her body. The fruitless efforts had exhausted her and she decided to conserve her energy instead. Now bobbing around without direction she was at a loss. Feeling like a rabbit trapped in headlights she had run out of options. It seemed she was here and here to stay. Fear rose in her as she stopped fighting the idea and allowed it to sink in.

There in the darkness loneliness took hold. Images of her children flashed before her tugging hard at her heart strings. Would she ever be with them again? She thought of her parents. They would be inconsolable preparing for their ultimate loss. She thought about Alex with a wave of love. This came crashing over her followed swiftly by the image of Jayne's face firing her up again with overwhelming anger. She felt her energy burn bright and forced herself to swallow the spectrum of feelings when the haunting echoes again signaled their ever presence. She wanted to sleep. To find some escape from this half existence. She allowed herself to drift off.

Louise sat crouched in the corner of the kitchen. She could smell the fabric softener scent lingering in the air from the washing machine opposite her. With a slight movement of her head the scent was replaced with that of cat food from the bowl on the floor. She gagged before using her foot to push the offending object out of nostril reach. She rocked gently back and forth wondering how it had come to this. Considering her next move, she wondered which one would be best.

The tablets the doctor had given her to calm her nerves made her thoughts foggy. Her thinking was now disjointed and no sooner had an idea presented itself, it seemed to evaporate. She was unable to maintain its thread to any adequate conclusion. The only image that was sustainable and frustratingly indelible was that of Colin. Colin and that whore of a woman! How dare she invade her life like that? Did she have no shame to cavort with someone else's husband? To disregard the existence of her little family unit. Bile rose in her throat. She could still smell that vile cat food. She forced herself to her feet. Unlocking the back door, she launched it through the air listening with slight satisfaction as it smashed to smithereens, pieces of china and food flying in all directions. Should she get dressed? What was the point it was almost five o'clock. Colin had taken the kids away for a few days to 'give her time to think'. Time to think! That was all she had been able to do since the bombshell. Try as she might to stop the whirling whys they were having a party in her head; an all night and all day party. The questions were driving her mad, stealing her peace and stealing her sleep. She couldn't escape them.

Colin was evasive. Evasive and elusive. Cowardice had always been in his nature. The affair had only highlighted this flaw in his character as he used their children as an excuse to run away from the fallout leaving her alone to pick up the pieces. She considered her limited options. *Leave?* How would she cope? She was in a state, that much was evident. They might try to take her children away from her. For their sake she reasoned that she must stay. If only she could find a way to stop all the bad feelings, the anger and the pure hatred that permeated her every pore.

Mia watched on as the vision played out before her with the clarity of a television screen. The kitchen layout seemed familiar. Seated there in *her* kitchen she wanted to reach out to the woman. Comfort her. She knew she couldn't. This time she knew she was merely an audience to this woman's predicament. She longed to tell her that she was free and with a little time and faith she could again feel whole and together. Well at least together enough to make a decision. Hopefully, the right decision. She could see she was trapped in a cycle of her own making, the negative spiral of thoughts circling her and trapping her in her very own ball of negativity. She was as trapped as surely as Mia was. Only Mia could see that this woman had the key to unlock herself and dissolve that invisible but powerful field that was encircling her. Mia wanted to scream at her *save yourself!* She couldn't reach her; she was merely an observer. Mia concentrated hard on the woman's face. Its features were indefinable and smudged; she concentrated her thoughts and slowly the features took shape and form. Devoid of any make up and stained with tears she recognized her immediately; it was Louise McKenzie! She could only watch as the woman in floral pyjamas curled into the foetal position and rocked herself accepting defeat before the flashback vision faded and melted away.

All was soon black again leaving Mia wondering if the vision had indeed just happened. She rationalized that she must have dropped off and been dreaming. A loud humming sound caught her attention. It stopped briefly only to start again. It continued for a few minutes; sounding ever closer before becoming more distant and then stopping. This cycle continued as if whatever was causing it were circling her; playing with her. Looking through the grazed chink that had become her window, she jumped in shock. Two massive black eyes were staring back at her, the black javelin antennae jabbed and jabbed at the ball, the ensuing tap-tap echoing, louder and louder with rippling vibration. The long suckered legs stuck fast to the shiny surface, the hairs so spikily close, she could see them clearly and its suit of green and blue armour shining metallic as it spewed its salivating juices. All the while those saucer sized empty ebony eyes threatening to devour her.

Relief washed over her as it gave up, she watched the rise of its translucent wings flutter and the tremendous hum of its take off. Expecting it to come back, she listened rigid with fear as the buzzing retreated into the distance.

28

Perry had that uneasy feeling again. It had been hanging around and he had taken to his bed for a couple of days, taking comfort from burying his head beneath the covers. During these times he looked at himself in disgust. Still, he had long since come to accept that this was part of who he was. That he would always need to emotionally shut down sometimes. Previous partners had not understood it. That was one of the perks of living alone now. Nobody to answer to. Nobody to worry that he was in some weird emotional turmoil. Nobody had been able to just accept that this was an overwhelming need in him. Normal. Well, normal to him anyway.

His work had thankfully brought him into contact with others like him. Artistic. Spiritually open people. They all shared similar experiences. Open on a level most people aren't, they sometimes found their batteries totally depleted. In the old days and more recently, when living with Adam, he had fought the urge to hibernate for a bit. Not anymore. He knew it was futile to fight what was to him an in-built instinct. Ignoring it merely led to a longer time to redress the balance.

At times like this he wondered what life was all about. To learn was the only answer that his years of pondering this question had come up with. Well it seemed to him that he was learning all right. Learning the same lessons over and over. He had learned them hadn't he? He thought so but then why did they keep coming over and over again?

There were occasional new ones, sure. Try as he might to figure it out, if he had really truly learned then why did the same lessons appear to keep coming around, again and again in his life?

Frankly he had had enough. Life had to him become an almost seemingly endless struggle. He didn't feel depressed. In fact he felt a clarity as clear as crystal. He had had enough. Of all this. He was eager and ready for the next 'thing' now.

Only it wasn't that easy. He didn't believe in suicide although he would be lying if he said that he had never considered it. He had. Several times. That was until a friend had gone down that path and he had seen first hand the devastation and destruction it caused to those that were left behind. He knew then that he couldn't do it.

In the bad times he indulged his imagination. What would he do if he were hit by a car? His life hanging in the balance would he find the strength to will himself back like stories of strangers he had heard about? Some cited love as their biggest motivation, they couldn't leave their families. Some told of a new found zest for life and an enthusiasm to fulfil their life's purpose whatever that might be. What was his?

He hadn't worked it out in spite of trying.

So he rode the bad times battening down the hatches until they passed, which inevitably, they always did. Until the next time. His belief system, unique to him as is everyone's, also informed him that the decision to take his own life was not really his to take; so he didn't make it. He plodded on strangely secure that this life would one day be over and done with. Finito. Just like that, with the seasons to come, his very existence would be washed away with time, all traces gone. Since he would finally be free one day, maybe a flutter in a cool summer breeze, he decided he would take his freedom now; whilst he was still in the driving seat, he might as well make the best of it.

Loneliness stabbed his guts. He had reached that point where he could no longer stand his solitude and yet he could no longer stand the intrinsic fakery of most people. Both mindsets had become intolerable to him. He had reached a stalemate within himself. He wondered again where Mia was. He could talk to her. She would understand. In her absence, he wondered who else he could talk to. There was no one.

He tried to stop thinking and turned off the bedside light as he prayed for sleep, even the one that he had every reason to believe he would awaken from the next morning.

29

The landscape within her circular prison seemed to change just as the kindly soul had told her. She began to understand that she could change it to some extent with her thoughts. Dreamscape was a better way to explain the surroundings she had found herself within and unable to escape. How had he come to be here? He was obviously capable of goodness as she knew she was. So how had she ended up here was probably a more pressing question? She thought back to the events before the blackness. She had remembered, the memories fleeting and cloudy, being overtaken with anger and nasty negativity.

The old lady from the train suddenly came to mind. She instinctively looked down at her hand remembering the burn. Only now, like that fast evaporating wound, her hand was no longer there. She lamented the loss of her body. The old lady's words came back to her 'reject negativity' only she hadn't. It had been all consuming culminating in her collapse that day in the kitchen. Full of anger and hatred she had allowed her good nature to be slowly chipped away until every last drop had been replaced with ill will and destructive emotions. It had happened without her being aware. Slowly at first but growing in velocity and volume it had grown out of control until there was almost nothing else.

She had played into Jayne's hands. She had known the power of the silver globe as surely as Mia had. How clever she had been in her game, the finale played out within sight of the witchball, that entrapper of all that is bad.

30

Feeling lighter Perry stood on the scales. He had lost four pounds. Funny he always did after, what his mother referred to as, one of his episodes. Lack of food maybe but he preferred to think that he had shed some bad energy shit. He felt lighter in spirit anyway not just in his body. This latest stint had been two days. He had switched off the phone. Not switched on the computer. Not eaten much. Not functioned in any normal sense of the world. He had checked all was well with family, let them know that he would be off the radar for a bit and took to his bed.

He soaped up in the shower washing away the remnants of the past couple of days. He used to feel guilt that he had given in to what to an outsider may look like laziness. He knew different and frankly was beyond caring what others thought of him. These periods were usually followed by a burst of creativity like somehow his mind shutting down and clearing away the cobwebs left space for something new and exciting. He just had to wait for it to come now he knew from experience that it was only a matter of time. He would stock up on supplies so that he could give whatever came, his full attention. He could hole himself in again and not have to bother with the banal things like going out and gathering food, well going to the supermarket, anyway. He felt energized and clean. Something was still niggling though. Something still didn't feel right.

He decided to take a trip into town and restock the fridge. He knew the pattern. His creativity was returning and he was looking forward to eliminating the nagging apprehension about Mia and going with the flow.

Arriving at the supermarket, he grabbed a trolley and made his way through the entrance. It was still early so hopefully he would be dodging the breeders and their wailing kids.

He swung the trolley up and down the sections grabbing bits here and there as he moved through the aisles. He tried to remember what he might fancy during his up and coming moments of creativity; could be anything. On that he knew that he had no pattern. He could fancy the most obscure thing, even things that he had usually disliked or never eaten before. Sometimes sweet. Sometimes savory. Shopping during these bursts more than overtook the money he had saved during the famine of the past couple of days. Finishing up as quickly as he could he fancied a doughnut and had to go back. Should he buy a box? If he bought a box he would surely eat the box. He bought the box relying on his willpower not to eat them all. He went straight back home and unpacked the shopping.

Back to reality he switched on his mobile. He had answerphone messages which he listened to on speaker. Packing the groceries away in the fridge he recognized Alex's voice. *Why was he calling?* In itself that was very unusual and there was something in his voice. Perry would call him back as soon as he packed the freezer stuff away. He opened the doughnuts.

Pearl had insisted on coming over and helping Alex put up the Christmas decorations just as Mia usually did every year. The kids had helped and they had seemed to enjoy the temporary distraction although Alex had found it all too much. Still, his mother-in-law was right, they had to put the kids first and do what was best for them to keep at least some semblance of normality. They didn't even want to stay in their own beds now preferring to go back and stay with Pearl and Herb. At least he had been able to finally get Jayne out of the house. He had not even offered her a lift home; since she had her bike he'd literally told her to get on it in more ways than one.

Just as he was about to return Alex's call, Perry's telephone rang. He recognized Mia's number immediately and picked up.

'Mia! Thank God. I have been worried about you,' a male voice interrupted him, stopping him mid-flow.

'Perry it's Alex.'

'Alex? What's happened is Mia ok?'

'She will be hopefully. She collapsed. She's in hospital.'

'She will be ok?'

'She's in a coma. They don't know what is wrong,' Alex's voice cracked with emotion, 'They are talking about us letting her go.'

Perry's stomach sank and there was a moment of silence as he digested Alex's words.

'Is there anything I can do?' said Perry finally finding his voice again.

'I don't know what to do mate. Can you tell me what to do?' Alex spoke in a voice weak with emotion.

'Alex,' Perry didn't know what to say, 'Alex don't lose hope. Hold on to her. Keep talking to her. I should come. Will it be ok if I come?'

'You can come. She thinks the world of you. Maybe if you speak to her. They say sometimes they can still hear.'

'Ok. Look I will get things organized and come just as soon as I can.'

'I don't know what's been happening. Weird stuff. I know you helped Mia. I know she told you about it. I have found some thing. Under the bed. A little bottle. It's filled with yellowy water and a nail. Do you know what it is Perry?'

'Keep it safe Alex. Look, we'll talk more when I come.'

The kids were staying at their grandparents again tonight. Alex felt better that Perry was coming but he hadn't given much away. He was sure that he knew what the bottle was. He would find out soon enough. In the meantime he made a sandwich, exhausted, it was his and Pearl's turn to sleep. Herb was taking the night shift tonight and had promised to call straight away if there was any change in Mia's condition. He gulped the sandwich down forcing it down his dry throat. He wasn't hungry. He poured himself a whiskey. He called Pearl. She answered in one ring.

'Pearl. It's Alex,' he spoke quickly, 'No news, just calling to make sure you and the kids are ok?'

'Yes we are all fine.'

'I can't help feeling I should be at the hospital.'

'We agreed. Herb will call. We need to get some sleep. You'll be there tomorrow. You'll be no use to us shattered. Now the kids are sleeping and I am off to get some sleep. Or try to at least. I suggest you do the same. Night-night.'

'Night Pearl.' He replaced the receiver.

Earlier, as he pulled the curtains, he'd knocked the little black cat off the windowsill. His searching hand had poked around blindly attempting to retrieve it from behind the headboard, puzzling when instead he had found the little bottle he now held in his hand. He couldn't sleep. He couldn't switch off his brain. He drank the whiskey and looked at the little bottle standing on the table. He shouldn't be drinking. He could be needed at the hospital at any time. Still he needed a drink and, deciding that he could always call a cab to the hospital, he poured another glass.

Switching on his laptop, he did a search on the bottle. He suspected it was some sort of ritualistic thing. Perry's reaction had reinforced this assumption. After all, he had not asked any questions and was not in the least bit forthcoming with information nor did he seem even the least bit curious.

There was his answer on the screen before him. It was a protection bottle. He was not able to protect her. She was trying anything to protect herself. She

had been truly frightened. He hadn't listened. His
anger rose again. It had never been far away since all
this had happened; an all consuming, destructive,
anger.

'Well what good did these do you Mia?' he
screamed as he launched the protection bottle
through the air in the direction of the ball.

He wailed as the bottle shattered the ball in a
twinkling silver eruption. Watching on in disbelief as
the bottle ricocheted against the stone wall and the
solitary nail shot out with all the focus of a bullet,
landing firmly and upright on the photo of Jayne, not
far from her heart.

It was dark and raining as Jayne cycled back to her
house. Alex had insisted she leave; he had practically
thrown her out the door, not even offering her a lift
this time since she had brought her bike. The little
lane was without street lamps and there was very little
moonlight to guide her. She was reliant on the light
on the front of her bike. It had started to flicker as
she turned into her road, blinking on and off, until it
finally ceased. She had travelled the road many times
and knew its very fabric, every bump and pothole.
She wasn't alarmed. Still she wanted to get home
quickly and started to peddle faster. She could see her
parked car now. She was almost home.

She felt the glass as she rode over it. The
handlebars shook in her hands as the front wheel lost
its traction. She couldn't control the bicycle as she
flew off bouncing once on her car bonnet before
being flung onto the fence like a rag doll. Opening
her eyes she saw and smelled grass and dirt. She

couldn't move her arms which were hanging limply at her side as she lay broken across the wooden fence. She felt something in her chest just as she passed out.

Coming to again, her upside down ears could hear dripping. She strained her eyes to see the liquid that was drip, drip, dripping as it formed its red puddle. Her silver shoes, the lovely sparkling pumps with the bows, were changing colour and turning red before her plate sized eyes.

Over at their house Pearl and Herb heard Grace start screaming in uncontrollable hysteria, 'My dog has gone! My dog!'

31

Mia heard the shatter of glass. The suction sensation was instantaneous. She exhaled hard, the force of which seemed to simultaneously force her eyes open. The room was empty of people although a high pitched beeping started immediately from one of the many machines in the room. She was back.

Suddenly there was a flurry of activity as medics filled the room. She was momentarily blinded as a doctor shone a bright torch in her wide eyes. She tried to talk but there was something in her throat. She felt the familiarity of physical pain again. She relished the discomfort; the perversity of this was not lost on her. Using her eyes she pleaded with the doctor to remove the tube. She had something to say.

'Calm down. You are safe. You are in hospital. We are looking after you,' said a nurse gripping on to Mia's shoulder as she tried to get up.

Mia needed to see her children. She needed to speak to Alex, to her parents. She needed to let them know of the danger that could be anywhere. She wasn't sure of what had been in that ball with her but it wasn't good. Like her, it wasn't there now. It could be anywhere. It was all around. It was everywhere. She was scared and scared for her children. *Where were they? Who was looking after them?* She suddenly felt dozy again.

Later she opened her eyes for a second time. Her mum's was the first face she saw. For a few seconds she considered if she was dreaming again. Was her mum here for real or was that kind face just a mirage created by her troubled mind?

'Mia!' cried Pearl, 'Oh Mia you are awake,' she said as the tears fell. She leaned across to hug her daughter.

Mia, feeling her mother's touch and smelling her familiar floral scent, finally accepted that she was really there and her eyes too filled with tears. She looked across to her father and smiled. He smiled back, his face slightly twisted as he tried to keep himself together for the sake of the two women.

'Alex is with the kids,' her mother had pre-empted the question that she couldn't ask.

'I'll go and call him,' said Herb leaning across he kissed his daughter on the forehead and whispered, 'We thought we'd lost you there girl.'

Herb escaped to the toilets; closing the cubicle door behind him he opened the floodgates in private. He looked up mouthing a silent thank you. Taking some toilet paper he wiped his eyes and blew his nose. Coming out of the cubicle he saw that he was not alone. Washing his hands their eyes met in the mirror. The other man looked down immediately averting his eyes. Herb said another silent thank you. He wouldn't have been able to cope if this stranger had shown him any sympathy.

He stepped outside the sliding doors and dialled Alex's number; he answered immediately. There was a moment of silence when he broke the news, as if Alex couldn't believe it or was doubting the truth of his father-in-law's words, if only for a brief second. He would be at the hospital as soon as he could.

32

Standing now in the shop doorway Peter looked out on the deserted street. The rain had stopped but the pavements were wet with puddles. The wind was kicking up a storm. It was getting dark now as the sun came down on the day. Not one single customer. No one was coming now. He looked behind him at the out of sync tick-tocking clocks. It was almost five. He shivered, the wind growling, as he stepped back inside to turn the shop open sign to closed, it knocked him off his feet. A mini whirlwind, black as black tornado. His eyes blinked as his mind didn't have time to process what he was seeing, it happened in seconds.

His aunt was ready. She knew something was coming. Her own demons were coming back to haunt her and she was ready and waiting for them. She heard the thump as they pushed past Peter. There was no time to check he was ok. The next sound she heard was the swooshing of the beaded curtain. Finding strength returning to her weak old limbs she stood to meet her destiny with dignity. She smelt them next. A putrid smell caught the back of her throat filling her nostrils.

It was then that she saw them. They had given her the gift of sight back to those violet eyes for the first time in nearly thirty years. Not in an act of kindness. What she saw made her wish she were blind again. Her seeing eyes widened with terror at the blackness and evil she had captured years before. Something had gone wrong. They had escaped. It was the last thought that crossed her mind as, with a petrified scream, she was devoured by the rotten stench of the blackness as she became part of it.

Florence was absorbed into the blackness. She was used to the blindness. What she was not familiar with was being part of the evil that now cloaked and choked her freed soul. Only it was not free. She recognized that she had been devoured by the badness. Her intrinsic goodness was no match. Still she fought to assert her true colours in the overpowering void of nastiness. Her struggling was futile. She was swept along on the wave of blackness. She heard the deep bellowing voice tell her to give up followed by a chorus of cackling laughter.

The night was dark without any trace of a moon. The mini black whirlwind spun through the shop letterbox causing it to clatter. Nobody heard as the vortex passed through the deserted street unnoticed. Overwhelmed Florence gave in to the feeling, becoming a passenger in the vehicle she could not escape. It was on a mission. Instinctively she knew that its target was Mia. She tried to blot out her memory of the girl, her goodness, her power and more importantly, her address. It was impossible. She knew that these demons were tapped into her psyche now. They were one and the same, her knowledge was theirs. Her memory would take them straight to her.

She felt encased in black treacle. Heavy and yet in some way she was being swept along as if part of some steamroller that threatened the annihilation of anything in its wake. In life she had learned not to show fear. Try as she might she was having trouble hiding it now. She had hoped to one day be reunited with Mia but not like this. The girl would stand no chance once the blackness came for her. She thought of Peter. Had his fragile being survived their arrival or was he still lying there on the shop floor, in pain or worse still dying, awaiting a customer that at this time of night would not come? No sooner had she thought of Peter in all his innocence and fragility than the vibration within the black formation seemed to falter and it changed direction. It was heading back to the shop.

Perry let the wind blow the cobwebs away. The sun was shining today although it was still cold when the bracing wind blew. His face tingled as the tiny grains of sand stung his skin. Breathing in the salty air, he felt alive. The stagnation of the past week fell way with every step. He picked up a piece of driftwood that had been carried in and spewed out on the high tide. Now discarded it lay drying in the sun. It was shaped like a penis. He laughed at the wonder of nature and considered the battering and weather that had given this piece of wood its distinctive shape. *What was it before?*

He would give it to Mia. She would appreciate it. Mia. She was back in the front of his mind again after hitching a ride at the back of his brain for the walk. He must see her, it was important. His face felt tight with the layer of salt and his ears were slightly numb. Still he had to admit he was feeling better if still a little uneasy. He must conquer his fear of going to the hospital. He couldn't work out whether it was really the fear of losing her. As the obstacles came, one after the other to stop him setting off, he couldn't deny that he felt relief. He was scared. She needed him and he couldn't let her down. He would be with her soon.

Stopping briefly back home to change his sandy shoes and pick up his wallet he was back in town within ten minutes. Luckily he found a parking space not far from the antique shop.

Glancing through the antique shop window as he passed by, it looked closed. He remembered this to be the first time that he had ever seen it closed. He looked up briefly to see the shopkeeper staring thoughtfully through the curved windows of the shop front. Perry nodded his head in recognition though the shopkeeper didn't seem to notice him. He thought of popping his head in and saying thanks; that Mia had been so pleased and happy with the witchball. Something in the shopkeeper's demeanor stopped him and he headed straight back to the car instead.

33

It had been late when the tick-tocking had brought Peter around. Rubbing his head he had felt confused. He remembered preparing to shut the shop early. He had noticed the clocks had all hailed five. Next thing he knew it was seven o'clock. Rousing himself he had called out to his aunt. There had been no answer and he had found her rigid near her chair behind the beaded curtain. He dismissed the time lapse as shock when the doctor had speeded over and pronounced her dead from probably natural causes. She was eighty seven after all. There was nothing suspicious. That was, apart from her violet eyes which were wide and the white of freshly veneered teeth; not the opaque of before so to make him wonder, for a fleeting moment, if it really was his aunt that lay before him. From the pained expression on her face they had speculated that it was probably a heart attack.

Peter had arranged the funeral on autopilot, the local undertakers had availability that same week. He

had utilized this numb time to the full calling up the
agent who had also found a buyer for the shop within
days. It was fast but Peter knew that it was what she
had wanted had she still been here. Only she wasn't.
He only had himself to look after now. He had
displayed a notice in the window informing their loyal
customers of his aunt's demise and of the shop
closing.

   Perry had seen the sign purely by chance. He
arrived at the graveyard early. This was his intention.
It had been a while since he had indulged his love of
graveyards. A few years ago, whenever he was feeling
low he had got into the habit of visiting graveyards.
Somehow he had found comfort in their very real
reminder that worry was pointless; for although we
may all take different paths and therefore experience a
multitude of different 'scenery' along the way,
ultimately this was where we were all headed. As his
spiritual awareness and belief in an afterlife had
developed and grown, the comfort the graveyards had
held somewhat receded. He had found himself
looking at them then merely as a place of rest for
worn out or discarded vehicles, specifically, bodies. A
sort of human scrapyard, a knacker's yard, with the
'vehicles' not piled high for reclaiming but buried low
in the ground, for their own special form of recycling.
He had kept this thought to himself. He was sure that
some might see it as distasteful and disrespectful. Life
had taught him to keep his more off the wall thoughts
to himself; people's feelings, particularly on this
subject ran high and he would hate to offend anyone.
If only people could be more open to the ideas of

others. Most in his experience were not, preferring to shut out such thoughts; to them, it seemed to him, to consider death made life too difficult to live. It had the opposite effect on him. Knowing that this place he was in now was the end of the line gave him a clearer perspective. He stood breathing in the peace. There was nobody else around and he said a silent prayer of gratitude.

He meandered through the headstones trying hard not to walk over any graves. For some obscure reason the thought of dancing on somebody's grave flashed into his mind. He wondered had anyone really ever done this to an enemy? He dismissed the hideous thought quickly. Knowing how nasty and vindictive people could be he was sure somehow that somewhere it would have happened. He respectfully kept his distance as he read the epitaphs. Some were worn away by the elements, some were covered and entangled with ivy. Some were lopsided and broken with the earth's subsidence.

He looked around him. The birds still sang, the trees flourished and flowers bloomed although death was all around. Out of the corner of his eye, he noticed the black skirts of the vicar's arrival. He considered going in to the church. He loved the quiet echoing within and the lingering smell of incense. He decided against it, instead leaving the small posy tribute just inside the door. He had written the card simply from himself and Mia. No religious words. No endearments. After all he hadn't known the old lady well and couldn't afford to be overly indulgent through fear of causing offence. Nor had he been able to tell Mia of the old lady's demise. He had only just seen the notice in the shop window and had come to pay his last respects on a whim. He had never met her but she had been kind and thoughtful to his friend and somehow it just felt the right thing to do.

He sat on the wooden bench *In Memory of William and Cecilia* and waited allowing his thoughts to wander. Not long after he heard clip clopping and looked up to see two magnificent black horses in full plume drawing the glass corsage. He stood and turned towards it as it passed, bowing his head in respect. What splendor. He felt a pang of regret that he had never met this woman in life for he was sure, that given the pomp and ceremony of her departure, they would have got on like a house on fire. Fire. Was she to be buried or cremated he wondered. He had noticed earlier a freshly dug and dressed grave beside an old and dancing willow. He hoped that would be this lady's final resting place.

He noticed some other mourners in distinctive black attire. It was only by chance that he himself had chosen a black shirt today for he had not expected to be here at this funeral. Following his recent low episode he had chosen it, always somehow feeling the protection the dark colour provided. He thought of Mia again. She had incorporated this idea into her everyday life by wearing only black underwear. His thoughts were so random today.

He spotted Peter. Should he go over and pay his respects? He was alone although surrounded by a handful of mourners. Perry wondered were they family?

A woman handed him an order of service which, out of politeness, he took. He now knew that, *Florence Renata Bridgestock 1923-2010*, was 87. She'd had a long life, looking around there were not many people of age there. He felt sadness that she had no doubt outlived her family and friends. He wanted to know more about the woman. He wondered if there were any other customers amongst the mourners. Maybe there would be a wake. Maybe he could take the opportunity to find out more about Florence and the life she had led. Maybe he could talk to Peter. Maybe they would become, in spite of their obvious differences, friends.

As Peter passed by all such thoughts diminished, in an instant. Overcome with a thick sense of sickness Perry instinctively stepped back. He had expected to pick up on Peter's sadness and pain. This was different. The grieving nephew appeared to be cloaked in some invisible funky hue which made Perry gasp. The pit of his stomach lurched as if he were suddenly on some sort of rollercoaster. He recognized the feeling. It was a mixture of petrified anticipation and doom. Only he had met Peter twice recently and his presence had never evoked such a sickening feeling before. Perry blinked, unsuccessfully attempting to break the hold of Peter's gaze, which held steadfast as he walked on by.

Winded, Perry headed back to the bench and sat down. He needed to catch his breath and centre himself again. There was no way he could go through with the service. He wondered how Peter would himself find the strength to enter that church in his present state.

Sufficiently recovered he made his way back to the car. He needed to get home quick and shut the door. He needed to work out what had just happened.

Driving home on autopilot he parked, locked the

car and got in the house as quickly as his jelly legs
would carry him. He closed the door, double locked
and slumped against it. His head was still splitting
filled with the fug of his encounter with Peter.

Instinctively he checked that the back door was
locked and systematically went around the house
checking all the windows. *Stupid.* This attempt to
ensure his apparently threatened security was, after all,
pathetic. He knew that. The almost tangible threat he
had detected had come from a source that would not
be phased by bricks and mortar.

The day was bright, the house illuminated in the
sunshine. The crystals hanging in the windows were
glinting, throwing colours of red and purple spheres
of light around the room.

He went around the house again pulling down
the blinds and closing the curtains. He needed to
block out the outside world again. Switching on the
lights in the kitchen and then, instantly thinking better
of it, switching them off again. He found some white
candles underneath the sink. Taking out a handful and
fixing them in various holders, he lit them in turn.

Taking a bottle of water from the fridge he sat
down at the table and drank the refreshing liquid. His
mouth was dry. He drained the bottle and took
another, this time a litre, from the fridge. He grabbed
a glass and sitting down with legs like jelly, poured
another glass of water. He had to pull himself
together. Alex was expecting him, relying on him and
he had to see Mia, she needed him.

The funeral was a quiet affair since most of
Florence's family and friends had already gone before

her. Peter recognized a few of their faces at the funeral. That common Londoner that took the witchball was there, albeit fleetingly but he was on his own, the flame haired woman wasn't with him.

Nobody had come back to the house. In fairness he had not pushed anyone to, preferring instead to sit alone with his thoughts. *The bitch was gone. Good riddance to her!* He had been gutting the house and wondering where the ill feeling now bubbling had come from. Aunt Flo had been good to him. *No! She had used him and held him back!* He'd sorted the valuable antiques into a pile then wondered why as he had accepted the first offer from the house clearance people. *Out with the old in with the new!* He had contacts, good contacts that would've given him a better price but that would've meant seeing them and enduring their sickening condolences. There was no time for that he had been locked up too long and had a life to lead!

Gorging himself with the finest food, wine and whiskey he tried to satisfy his uncharacteristic insatiable appetite. After two days of none stop eating his mind switched on to the next base need. Sex. He turned to prowling the bars, chatting up anything in a skirt with compulsive wild abandon. Some of the women he approached silently sneered. Some told him outright to get real and leave them alone. All of them in some way turned their noses up to this weird looking, musty smelling, time warped dressed man. The final straw came when, on one such night, he was tapped on the shoulder and told to leave, he was drunk and making a nuisance of himself and upsetting the women. Seconds later and forcibly removed, he found himself out on the street. All the alcohol had gone straight to his head. He rarely drank. As he headed home he saw a lone female walking ahead. Hearing his footsteps she turned around, a slight fear etched on her face. It was dark and the street was deserted. Peter felt an overwhelming urge that he must have her. He would take her by force if necessary. In that split second he felt confusion. What was going on he had never desired a woman before. Yet this feeling was gathering momentum within him and it felt like a force beyond his control.

As the cab passed, the young woman frantically flagged it down silently counting her blessings and thanking God for her luck. Peter was overcome with a strange feeling of frustration and anger. He knew he had to get home. His aunt's death had had a strange effect on his emotions and he was no longer sure that he was in charge of them. He felt rather the opposite, that they were at this moment, clearly in the driving seat.

He spent his time fighting the contradictions. By some mysterious fluke, fuelled by his need for food, he mastered the internet and had groceries delivered. He grew fat. He ordered porn. His days passed in gluttony and sloth. Fighting the urge to go out for on some level he knew that it could be catastrophic as he didn't know or trust himself anymore. Growing fat, as the days passed, until his trousers no longer fitted he had ordered more with his next shop. The day they arrived he binged before slipping them on. Looking at his new rotund shape in the mirror the voice in his head chastised *'You look disgusting! You have no spark, no energy. Who would want to be with you, you sad pathetic loser'*, his demons taunted him.

34

Perry rose early in preparation for the long drive to Mia. He had dilly dallied for long enough, it was time to face the music. Bending down he picked up the pile of post and the paper on his way back up to the bathroom. Still wearing his bathrobe, he sat on the bed, finishing his coffee and flicking through the newspaper. It was then that he saw it. The e-fit. He knew this identikit likeness. Something about the man's face was familiar. A little fatter maybe. A little more weathered with more facial hair but very familiar. He mulled it over not being able to place the face. He read the headline and learned that the man in question was wanted by police in connection with their enquiries into a very serious attempted assault. No he couldn't know this vile thug. Maybe just someone that he had come across down the pub.

The thought hit him like a lightning bolt. This wasn't someone he had seen at the pub. This was the witchball guy. The man from the closed down antique shop.

Perry peered closer to study the features. He had
to be sure. This was one serious allegation and the
poor guy had only just buried his aunt. No. Couldn't
be him. Must be a coincidence. Perry thought that
maybe he should just let the police know. Just in case.
No. He couldn't do it. The poor bloke had only just
lost his aunt and his livelihood. Talk about things
coming in threes. No Perry couldn't do it to him.
Surely this was just a case of mistaken identity.
Anyway if he had thought it himself then surely some
one else, another customer from the shop perhaps,
would have thought it too. Let them be the one to do
the dirty deed. The poor guy had enough on his plate,
Perry had seen that first hand at the funeral. He for
one did not want it on his conscience to dob in an
innocent guy. Could be the final thing to tip him over
the edge. He decided to quash the idea and get
dressed. He still needed to finish packing and stop in
the garage for petrol.

Arriving at the garage soon after he filled up and
grabbed a basket for some munchies for the journey.
As he made his way through the entrance he came
first to the newspaper and horrid plastic tasting
sandwich section. There, staring out at him, was the
face again. It really did look like the antique shop guy.
Perry couldn't deny it.

35

Peter passed wind loudly. He laughed. His usual good manners had been replaced with that of a heathen. He drowned the last dregs from the can of pop, letting out a rattling belch. Laughing again, he got up. His stained jogging bottoms, with the elasticated waist, were even getting tight now. The top of his legs chafed. Putting his hand down into his pants he scratched his balls, rearranging his furniture, fighting off the urge to sniff his hand. *'Manners maketh man'* he heard his mother's voice in his head. *'Shut up!'* said another voice. He must be spending too much time on his own. The voices wouldn't leave him alone.

He pulled the curtains for the first time in days letting in the light. Cracking open a window slightly he looked around the room. Discarded food wrappers, cans and unwashed plates were strewn everywhere.

'You slob!' for once this internal voice was his own.

Grabbing some bin liners from beneath the kitchen sink he started to clean the place up. One plate was so encrusted with a week old take away that he binned that too. It made him gag. He was sure that the place stank. Emptying the ashtray he wiped away the overspill of ash and butts from the table. He had recently discovered a liking for smoking too. He cleared away the empty booze bottles. The smoking and drinking had given him acid reflux and as he stood up from the table his throat filled with burning bile. Quickly swallowing it back down again, he resolved to knock these recently acquired bad habits on the head. Since his aunt had gone he had seemed to be on a passage of self-destruction.

He picked up the pile of dirty magazine. The top one was entitled Minge Magnets. He couldn't look at the other titles but they were definitely 'specialized' and covered a weird and wonderful range to get your rocks off to. He picked up the pyramid pile of tissues between one finger and thumb placing them in the bag. The sick rose in his throat again as he felt pure and utter disgust. He tried to remember where had he purchased this wanking material? Online surely. He must have been blotto; he couldn't remember. He racked his brains; had he been out? *Please let me remember* if only to save the embarrassment of going to that newsagent again. He had locked the doors and hidden the keys from himself. How silly it sounded now. He couldn't find them. *No matter they will turn up.*

He went to the front door to see if there was any post. The missing keys were there in the lock. He was sure he had not left them there. He must have been out and put them in the door to lock it on his return. Only he couldn't remember. He picked up the post and the local paper. From the date he noticed that he had been holed up for more than a week. At least he thought he had. He sat down and through the drunken haze of the past few days he strained his memory. Nothing. It was then he spotted himself staring back out at him from the front page of the newspaper.

Trying to make sense of what had happened, the words of the article started to swim before his eyes, only a few registering. Well built. Scruffy. Old fashioned style of dress. It certainly looked like him. He had to be honest with himself. The way that he had recently let himself go it certainly sounded like him too. Although the old fashioned style of dress seemed a bit unfair. He had only bought those trousers online recently. *Bloody hell! Shut up!*

Concern about the way he looked was the least of his problems. He concentrated, focusing his eyes. "Attempted rape". The words made his heart skip a beat. This was serious. He closed the window and drew the curtains. This was serious! The e-fit looked like him. The police would come. Too many people knew him from the shop. His face was well known. Well at least his skinny frame face was well known. Maybe people wouldn't recognize him. Was it him? He had never in his life had facial hair before. Neither had he ever carried this much weight. It certainly looked like him though, there could be no denying. Holding up the paper to his face, he peered into the mirror.

'Fuck!' as he said the word he winced.

He never swore. Then again so much of his behavior of late was alien to him.

'The pigs are coming to get you'. The voice laughed

inside his head. *'You are going down fat man. And you're on your own'*.

He looked around the room. The bottles. The mess. The filth. Then the events of his nightly prowl flicked out like a film in his head. He felt revulsion. What had got in to him? He found the bottle of tranquilizers the doctors had given him to help after his aunt's death and, taking them with him to the bathroom, quickly finished tidying up.

He took a bath. Picking up the razor he thought twice about removing his beard. He would leave it. Give them no doubts when they found him that he was their man. He dressed again in clean clothes. He combed his hair. Taking the tablets from the bedside cabinet, he caught sight of the picture again on the newspaper lying there. He repulsed himself. That was it. He swallowed the first handful of tablets. *'No!'* the voice screamed. His hand shook as he attempted to shake more tablets from the bottle spilling some onto the floor. He felt an overwhelming need to stop. Maybe his body would cope and expel the poison he had just taken.

He must find Mia. His head started to swim.

'Aunt!' he called out, settling back on the freshly laundered sheets of the bed he closed his eyes. A feeling of peace descended. *She was there*. He opened his eyes and in a flicker he thought he saw her standing at the foot of the bed, smiling at him. Her vision gave him strength and he swallowed two more handfuls with difficulty, defying his gullet which was fighting against performing its reflex. *God forgive me*. He fought hard against the urge to go to the bathroom and make himself sick. *Let this be an end to it* he begged, his words a silent plea within his head.

He felt a heavy painful pressure building within him followed by an inaudible popping sensation. With his final gasping intake of breath he watched as the black mass rose from within him and headed through the bedroom door.

Closing his eyes, relieved that it was all going to be over, he fell asleep.

36

Endless tests later Mia was finally discharged. She hadn't slept. She couldn't. She had been allowed to go to the family room yesterday to see the kids; at last that awful waiting and feeling of longing was over. She hugged them tight and didn't want to let them go. Somewhere deep inside she knew that life would never be the same again. She had spoken of her visions and experiences with her parents. They had assured her that these were normal, that others in a coma had recalled this near death phenomena. She waited for her mum to leave the room before taking the opportunity to talk more to her father. She felt safe to do that. He was a wise man and had an open mind. Not like her husband who would make the right noises before later telling her that she had fallen off her rocker and should pull herself together.

'I don't think I was dreaming Dad.'

'What else could it have been Mia.'

'Dreams fade. These thoughts, these feelings they are vivid. Like they really happened.'

'Well in a way they did happen didn't they? You have not been here Mia. Your body, yes that was lying in that bed, but you, your spirit, your soul whatever you want to call it, that was somewhere else. Away with the fairies.'

'Do you think I am mad Dad?'

'No,' he grabbed his daughter's hand to comfort her, 'What's this all about Mia?' He waited, pausing to give her time to answer but she said nothing. 'Look you need to stop trying to understand everything Mia. Some things are just too big for us to understand,' he went on, 'I can remember dreams from years ago. Years ago. There was one, me and Debbie Harry were stranded on a desert island.'

'Dad!' she smiled knowing that he was trying to make her feel better, 'This wasn't a dream Dad. Honestly. You do believe me?'

'Does it matter what I believe Mia?'

'Yes. Yes Dad it matters to me. More than you can ever know.'

'I know that you are not a liar Mia. Even when you were a little girl, you never resorted to lies. So yes, if you need an answer to your question Mia, I believe you.'

'I think I am in danger Dad.'

'Nothing is going to harm you. I won't let it.'

'Dad,' Mia was unsure of just how much to reveal to her father. She was not a little girl anymore and she knew, even if he didn't yet, that this was not something that he could make better with some well placed words and a cuddle, 'Can we come home?'

'Yes we thought that you would. So that Mum and me can help with the kids until you get back on top form again. We already spoke about it with Alex.'

'I am leaving him Dad.'

'What? Don't be daft Mia.'

'I've made up my mind.'

Pearl came back into the room.

'Mia is coming home with us love.'

'Oh good, Dad managed to persuade you then?'

'No I didn't have to.'

'You and Alex can have the front bedroom and the kids can have the box room we'll make do for a bit.'

'Alex is not coming.'

'What do you mean? He's coming soon,' she checked her watch, 'Not long now, he will be here by two. He is bringing some clothes and your things you are going to need.'

'Like he knows what I need. Don't make me laugh.'

Herb and Pearl looked at each other and Pearl went and sat on the edge of the bed.

'The doctors said that you may feel a little off sorts. You know, confused, before you find your feet again Mia. We know this is not really you talking. You can shout and scream and take it out all out on us Mia.'

'That is what we are here for love,' added Herb.

Mia wanted to scream. They were not listening to her. Did they think that she was suddenly unable to make decisions? That she had woken up no longer knowing her own mind? She couldn't find the strength or the inclination to argue with them now. She was grateful for their concern and support. She was going to need them and who was she to shout and scream, hadn't they been through enough these past few days too? She decided to stay silent and hugged them both in turn.

'Thank you,' she said 'but I need to go home. To my home I mean. There are some things there I need to pick up. Dad, would you tell Alex not to worry? Maybe you could take me there later, after we have settled the kids in.'

'But,' attempted Pearl.

'No buts,' Herb stopped her mid-flow, 'if that's what Mia wants, that's fine with me. I'll let Alex know. You get ready here. I'll call him now. Be back in ten minutes to help you to the car.'

Mia kissed her father. She always knew that she could rely on him. He was the only man that she had ever known that had never let her down. Ever. She knew that she could rely on him now.

'All ready?' Pearl picked up Mia's bag.

'Yes Mum. It may not be easy Mum but I am really going to need your help.'

'We are here Mia. Always. Why don't you leave the kids with us and stay with Alex at yours tonight?'

'No,' Mia was adamant, 'I don't want to be separated from the kids and me and Alex are done. I want nothing more to do with the arsehole.'

'Mia!' Pearl chastised, 'You don't mean that. It's ok the doctors said this would happen. It'll take a little time to get back to normal, that's all.'

'This is nothing to do with what happened!' said Mia thinking that it had everything to do with it and, what she had seen when she was trapped there in the witchball, watching him and that harlot. Was she going mad? Had she seen what she thought she had seen? Or was it just the taunting of her troubled mind trying to make sense of the senseless situation it had found itself in? Momentarily suspended like that, had her imagination played those images in her head? They had felt so real, surely they must have happened? Ben had seen her. He had waved to her. Was that real or just another playing reel from her delusional mind? She must be going crazy.

She had to get out of this hospital. If she wasn't careful she was sure that it wouldn't be too long before she was in another hospital. One with padded walls, just like she had been shown visions of. Her fears were only one step away from becoming reality if she kept thinking like this. Her mum was right. She had to give herself time. Only, after her coma, time had taken on such a different significance. Or more to the point, she had begun to wonder if time played any significance at all. Nothing made sense anymore.

Mia dialled Perry's number.

'Perry it's Mia.'

'Mia?' Perry was finally in the car and ready to set off to see her on her deathbed and she was calling him. *What was going on?*

'Perry I am ok. I need to see you. Alex said you told him you were coming.'

'I am.' Perry composed himself knowing that he should have gone to her sooner, 'It's good to hear you Mia. I am on my way. I should be there tonight.'

'Maybe you should stay there. I need to get away and think. I was thinking that maybe I could come and stay with you again. Just for a bit?'

'You should be resting Mia. You need to be with your family. Be taken care of. I can come to you.'

'Please Perry I need to think.'

'What about the kids?'

'I can't be with the kids right now. It's not safe. Mum and Dad will watch them. Just until I sort things out.'

'What about Alex? Look Mia I think you need to be with him and the kids.'

'Please Perry! You have to listen I am in danger! I can't keep them safe. I don't want them with me until I know that I can protect them.'

'Ok ok. What do you want me to do?'

'Stay put. Just until I call you.

'Ok. Well let me know as soon as you can. You feel ok?'

'I don't know how I feel. Mad?'

Back at her parents' Alex and the kids were waiting. Grace had to be coaxed to say hello to her; that hurt. Her mother had explained it away that her little mind probably felt that she had been left by her mother. Kids didn't understand and they'd had to prepare Grace for the possibility that her mummy was going to heaven. She was just confused that was all. Mia smiled but didn't really believe this to be the case. Alex said very little. She knew from his face that her visions were real. She felt his guilt. It was all she needed to give her the impetus to carry out her decision to leave. She would wait and bide her time. She didn't have the energy to fight with him anymore. She would present it to him as a fait accompli. This time he had no choice. His time for choices had passed when he had succumbed to temptation. She found the Goldilocks book to read to Grace later knowing she had some making up to do to restore the trust and influence of that woman's unwanted presence in her daughter's life. Shame the same principle couldn't be said for her marriage. She had to be honest with herself, that time in the ball had taught her nothing if that. She no longer wanted to be with him and his weaknesses. She needed all her strength for herself now. She knew that there was trouble ahead. She bathed and kissed Ben, putting him to bed. She read Grace the story and said goodnight.

'I am here Grace. Mummy's here.' She wanted to tell her daughter that she would never leave her again but she didn't want to lie to her. She had the feeling that there was going to be a time when again she would not, could not, be there for her. She went back downstairs.

'Ready to go love?' said Herb.

'I'll take her Herb,' said Alex.

'If that's what Mia wants?' looking at his daughter.

'It's ok Dad. I'll go with Alex,' she felt bad setting up conflict between the two men when they had always got on, 'Will you pick me up later please Dad?'

'If that's what you want.'

'What do you mean? I can bring you back. I'm coming back. With you I mean.'

'See you later,' Mia said to her parents, ignoring him.

In the car Alex asked her what was going on.

'You've got to be kidding me.'

'No. No. I am not. Mia! I deserve an explanation.'

They went into the house. Mia went straight upstairs and, pulling out a suitcase from the top of her wardrobe, she started to pack as Alex watched on.

'I owe you nothing. We can stay civil for the

kids.'

'What the hell do you mean?'

'I am done Alex. It's finished. Over. I know what you did.'

'What I did? What the fuck are you talking about? My God I know you have been ill but what's all this about Mia? Tell me! Please! I am going out of my mind.'

'Change of tactic eh? No I am the one that went out of my mind. Remember?'

'Look we need to work through this stuff. We can make things right again. I know I could've been a better husband. I should have been there for you Mia.'

'No it's ok Alex. You were right. I went mad… out of my tiny mind. You were right.'

He followed her, trying to take the case for her. She was having none of it. Opening the suitcase on Grace's bed she began to add her daughter's clothes.

'No I was wrong Mia. There. I said it. I was wrong.'

She ignored him and went into Ben's room grabbing the tiny sets of clothes from the wardrobe and drawers. She threw a few toys on top of the clothes making use of all the available space before zipping up the case and made for the stairs.

'Let me carry the case. Mia stop. I know you are angry. The doctors told us that it may be some time before you are normal again.'

'Normal!'

'Well the same. Not normal. You know what I mean,' he tried to explain, 'like you were before.'

She left the suitcase at the top of the stairs and he grabbed it, following after her.

'No Alex. Things will never be the same as they were before. Something changed.'

Walking into the kitchen she stopped. Hundreds of pieces of silver glimmering glass covered the floor. As she flicked on the light they created twinkles across the carpet.

'What the hell?'

'It was an accident. I meant to clear it up but it's been the last thing on my mind the past couple of days.'

'The ball smashed?' Mia looked on, her mind suddenly bursting with questions. 'How? When? When did it smash Alex?'

'I don't know, yesterday, the day before? What does it matter, when?'

'Think! It is important. When?'

'Just before I got the call to come to the hospital.'

'Which call?'

'What?'

'Which call' she screamed at him.

'When Herb called,' thinking hard now 'He called to tell me you had come around. I went to the hospital straight away. Look I'll clean it up now. Be careful you don't cut yourself.'

He misread the horror in Mia's eyes as she realized that this was just another very real sign that her dream was in fact a frightening reality. She had been in that witch ball. And when it smashed she had been set free...along with whatever else it held.

'It's only a ball love.'

'Only a ball!' she had to sit down her legs suddenly felt like jelly.

'I'll find you another. If it means that much to you. I promise. I will find you another.'

'How did it happen?'

'What do you mean?'

'You know what I mean Alex. I wanna know how it happened. How did it smash? Freak gust of wind?' She was being sarcastic now, she knew that he had put it up carefully and that it wasn't going anywhere without a bit of help.

He paused considering lying to her that the door had slammed. No she wouldn't buy it and there had been enough lies lately. He prepared to tell the truth. 'I smashed it,' he spoke slowly, 'I was drunk and angry. It was stupid. I threw a bottle at it.'

She noticed the empty whiskey bottle on the table. It was then that she spotted the photos. The happy snap of her and Alex, Grace and Ben. Her happy little family.

She glanced across at the other photo. It was of her happy little family too. Only she wasn't in this one. As she picked the print up it ripped. She held the jagged piece containing the image of Alex and her two children. The other part of the photo was ripped, the other torn piece held fast by a nail on to the wooden table. Frowning, she looked closer to see Jayne and the head of the offending nail embedded between her ample breasts.

Finding the dustpan and brush Alex started to sweep up the remnants of the witchball. He'd left in a hurry for the hospital and, because the kids hadn't been home since, he'd been in no hurry to clear it up. Holding the torn photo Mia shouted at him to stop.

'Ok! Ok!' He couldn't do right for doing wrong.

'I am leaving you Alex.'

'Look you don't know what you want right now. I understand. You need time.'

'You are not listening to me.'

'Please tell me what you want me to do me. I will do it. Anything to make things right. I just want things back to how they were before.'

'Before?' she spoke slowly, 'Before what?'

Looking down he picked up the remains of the little protection bottle, placing it on the table. Much of the thick glass had survived; only the jagged edge of the tapered neck was broken, its cork and contents set free on impact, 'Before all this madness started.'

A few minutes passed in silence.

'Maybe we should move.'

'Move?'

'Everything was fine before we came here. Maybe it's the house?'

Mia listened.

'Maybe this is an unhappy house,' he continued, 'You said yourself some places are just unhappy. Maybe this place is one of them.'

'It's not the house that's unhappy. 'It is me that's unhappy Alex. I think we should separate.'

'And just give up?' he was pleading now, 'How can you just let it all go Mia?'

'Maybe I just don't feel we have anything left.'

'But we have, we are a family. We'll get through this Mia.'

'It's too little too late Alex,' she spoke the words quietly 'I just don't have anything to give anymore. I am sorry Alex.' She glanced around the shining shards covering the floor. Looking at the broken protection bottle she wondered how it came to be in the kitchen.

He watched as she walked out to the hall, dialled the telephone and asked Herb to come and pick her up.

'I am going to stay at Mum and Dad's for a few days.'

He knew her well enough to know that, when she had made up her mind, she was adamant. He wanted to ask her about seeing the kids. Dare he say it, access. Just the thought stopped in its tracks, too hideous to think that he could fast be coming one of what his father-in-law called, fast food dads. He could only watch her as she got into Herb's car and it pulled away. She would never stop him seeing the kids. She would never try, he knew that. The finer details could wait. With any luck she would come to her senses and be back home soon.

He cleared up the remnants of the shattered witchball. It clattered as he emptied the dustpan into the bin. He vacuumed the final tiny shards up. Switching on all the lights he lay down on the floor searching for any stray twinkles. There were none.

Pulling out a chair from the table he sat down and removed his socks. He walked every inch of the area bare footed. Better that he trod on any bits he may have missed than the kids. He was sure that Mia would soon come to her senses and that they would all be together again soon. He would tidy the place and concentrate on that thought. He couldn't allow any doubt to creep in. Life without them was not worth contemplating.

Sure that he had not missed any broken glass he switched off the lights and went upstairs to bed. Tossing and turning the events of the past few weeks ran like a loop in his mind. He couldn't sleep. He couldn't make sense of anything. He thought about Jayne. Nothing had happened. At least he didn't think it had. It had seemed so real at the time. He had been tempted sure. He had almost fallen under her spell but he had resisted. There was no way that Mia could know. As real as it seemed he was sure it was only a dream. She was just letting her imagination run away with her. Maybe Jayne had been stirring things. Maybe she had been to see Mia. He couldn't fathom when she might have had the opportunity. He berated himself again for his foolishness.

He typed out a text to send to Mia. He spent an age thinking about what to say. He typed. He deleted. Again and again. This was stupid. She was his wife. He was her husband and yet he was unsure of what to say to her. He had so much to say a text seemed inadequate. Cheap even given the gravitas of the situation. He settled on *I will wait Mia. Forever if I have to. I love you. Come home x* He hit send and tried to sleep.

37

Back at her parents' Mia said goodnight. She went into the little box room with its single bed and pulled the curtains. The kids were sleeping soundly next door, her mum and Grace taking the double bed. How strange it felt to be back at home with her parents again. Her mind was racing. She knew that she wanted some distance from Alex but she was unsure of her next move. She felt up in the air. Unsettled. The little bed felt strangely small after so many years of sleeping in a double. She hoped she would not have another lucid dream tonight. She hadn't mentioned her dreams to her parents. She wasn't aware if Alex had. Maybe they had spoken about the strange occurrences when she was out for the count. If they had nobody had mentioned it to her. She flicked off the light.

She woke in panic struggling to breathe in those few moments that follow when the comforting realization dawns that it was only a dream. Woken mid-flow she clearly remembered her dream. It was

vivid. The lady statue had come to life and was having
a fight with the gargoyle in the garden. She had
watched it play back in her head as a reflection in the
silver of the witchball. In the senseless world of
dreams the gargoyle had grown a body and was using
the chain of the ball to strangle the lady statue. She
had woken up feeling a tightening around her neck.
Her imagination was on overdrive. Wide awake now
she was too scared to even close her eyes; and scared
too, to keep them open.

She was still tossing and turning when the birds
started their songs outside. A glint of sunshine came
through the chink in the heavy curtains. For a split
second she was back in the witchball the sliver of
silvery brightness dazzling her weary eyes disturbing
the otherwise darkness of the room.

She needed to make some decisions. She lay
there for a few minutes pondering. Should she wait
and see what unfolded? Perhaps now was not the
right time to make important life changing decisions.
She remembered the words of a former boss,
'Remember doing nothing is also an action'.

Those words of wisdom came bounding back
towards her now. She knew herself well enough to
know that she was always one to take action. Perhaps
she should heed those words now for they had come
to mind for a reason. Her resolute self took charge.
No. She would not stand and watch her life unravel.
She would make the decision; tough as she knew this
would be. She took a pen and paper and, deciding the
bright sunshine was too much for her morning eyes,
switched on the bedside lamp. She started to outline
her options. The kids were her priority; she needed to
make sure that they were safe. Her parents would,

eventually at least, support her decision whatever it may be. For now she decided, without a moment's hesitation, that she would ask them to mind the children and that they would do so. She would tell Alex that he could have access whenever he wanted she would not, could not even, entertain the idea of depriving him of his children, nor them of him.

She wanted to see Perry. He would understand and help her work out her head. She wished she hadn't told him not to come now. She desperately needed to talk to him about what had happened. He would not judge her, deem her to be unstable or mad; she couldn't risk talking to anyone else about it, not even her parents. Not just because of the weirdness of it all but because she sensed that such knowledge may put them in some sort of danger. She knew with absolute certainty she would not talk of it to Alex. In that moment she recognized the chasm that had formed in her marriage. She was sure he would ship her out to the funny farm. She decided to book a ticket to Cornwall as soon as possible.

She spoke to her parents over breakfast and got the kids ready. Grace had been distant and grizzly since her return. She was crying almost non-stop and repeatedly asking for a dog again. Hers, she had explained to her grandad, had gone. Her mother had relayed the story to Mia explaining that the imaginary pet had not been around since they had all been called to Mia's hospital bed. Pearl explained it away as the little girl's way of coping, her tiny unformed mind preparing herself for what she thought was her mother's imminent death, by practicing these untread emotions in the first instance with her imaginary pet. Mia knew that there was more to it than that but said nothing.

Grace had seemed frightened by her mother's return. She kept her distance and Mia was at a loss as to how to bridge the gap which had also formed between them. She decided that perhaps now was not the time to try. As much as it hurt she stepped back and let her child, her little girl, for the moment be comforted by her own parents. Baby Ben was unaffected. He was too young to understand. She cuddled him safe in the knowledge that the memories of this time would fade as the years passed. Grace was not so lucky. Mia wondered how Jayne had infected her fragile little being. She knew that she had. In time maybe she would know how much. She wanted to know but for the sake of her daughter hoped that, as she grew, these things would too become faded memories for her little girl.

She thought back to her earliest memories. She was sure that she could remember being five although specific memories of this time remained elusive. Her clearest memories were of being seven and eating ice creams in the warmth of the heat wave of 1976. She remembered her dad saying that he could remember way back and he even recalled memories of sitting in his pram. She prayed to God that memories of anything bad Grace had seen would leave her but she knew that they wouldn't. All that it took for the memory to be forever etched was for it to be so real, so totally out of the ordinary, so frightening. She knew that her little girl had been frightened. She resolved to find Jayne and work out what had been going on. But first she would call into the house and tell Alex of her plans.

After a fitful night Alex rose early. He had an overwhelming urge to see Jayne. He needed to tell her how stupid he had been and how he was going to fight for his family. He wanted to hear it from her that she would stop her attempts to meddle in his marriage.

He knocked on her cottage door. There was no answer, it was all shut up. Catface appeared and circled his feet. She was meowing loudly. He got back in the car and noticed the yellow police sign in front of Jayne's car. Must have been an accident? He thought no more of it and decided to call into Fred's shop on the way to Herb and Pearl's. He needed to see Mia and he needed to see his kids.

Fred was, as usual, working the tills.

'How do Alex, what you after today? Not seen you for a while heard the wife has been poorly.'

'Um it was touch and go there for a bit Fred. She's back home now.' He decided not to go into the finer details.

'Good to hear. Still after that popcorn? Got plenty in.'

'No. Not today,' said Alex grabbing the kids' favourite sweets, 'On second thoughts, go on, I will take a bag of that popcorn.'

'Second shelf along,' Fred gestured. 'Last time you came in for this Jayne had cleared me out. Terrible thing. Not my favourite person but not a nice end.'

Alex looked puzzled.

'You not heard then?'

'Heard what? What's happened? I saw the police sign on the way through.'

'She's dead Alex. Came off her bike. Impaled her

on the fence, rusty nail through the heart,' Fred stopped talking to serve another customer whose ears had pricked up at the whiff of some juicy gossip. Alex watched on stunned. When he was finished Fred continued, 'Terrible death. They say she was there all night. Long enough for a spider to make a web across her face anyhow. Bled to death.'

Alex listened, horrified.

'Well it's a dark lane at night. Any passing cars wouldn't have seen her. She was hidden, trapped behind her car.'

'I can't believe it,' said Alex, 'Catface. I just saw her cat.'

'Where?' said Fred.

'I just came by her place like I said. Someone needs to look after the cat. It must be pining. And hungry.' Alex went to get some cat food, 'Poor thing must be hungry, was miaowing like crazy.'

'Must have been,' Fred paused, 'if you heard it from the car.'

Alex paid and made his way back to Jayne's house. He felt sick. Catface appeared as he ripped open the cat food and put it in an old bowl he found on the floor. The smell made him heave. He sat at the patio table where just days before he had left the gargoyle. The wind blew a second tranche of the foul smelling food and he was physically sick. He waited a few minutes, took another seat down wind and watched the cat eat with fury. Pulling himself together he saw the tin watering can, just as Catface started to sniff at his vomit contemplating a second course. Filling the can from the outside tap he proceeded to wash it all away, clearing the stray lumps with a broom. He still felt nauseous. What should he do about the cat? Would someone come? Relatives? Jayne had not mentioned family but he suspected that she'd had no children. He thought about taking the cat with him to Pearl's. It was out of the question. For a start Herb was allergic. And Mia. Well Mia would go apeshit if he turned up with Jayne's cat. Should he take it to the cat sanctuary? She was scratching madly at the front door now.

He decided he should go to see his family as planned and come back later to see if Catface was still abandoned. He would bring her more food. He found an old plate underneath a flower pot and filled it with water so she had something to drink. Patting her on the head, she hissed at him. Charming he thought. She looked different. He was beginning to doubt if this mangy looking feline before him was Catface. Her glowing eyes lit up like transparent pools as they caught the light, the whiskers above them too long and arc like. She hissed again revealing the longest fangs he had ever seen on a cat this size. The whiskers around her mouth were also too long and in the style of a Fu Manchu moustache. This was not the domesticated cat he had met before. Still he told it that he would be back later. His voice sounded somehow loud to him in the quiet of the garden and he felt slightly stupid talking to a cat that had just turned on him. As it turned and walked away he wondered why he was bothering; tail tall in the air, arsehole exposed for all to see, its silent air of 'fuck you' was complete with this perfectly formed exclamation mark.

His mouth tasted of sick he needed a drink himself. Perhaps he should call in Fred's again, grab a drink and ask him what he thought about the cat.

'Miss me already eh Alex?'

Alex forced a smile and grabbed some more cat food, a fizzy drink and some chewing gum.

'I fed the cat. Do you think it will be alright?'

'I don't know. Probably feral anyway.'

'That would explain it going for me. Talk about biting the hand that feeds you. Did she have any family, any friends?'

'No' answered Fred shaking his head.

'Really. But I thought she had lived here for ages.'

'She has always been here.' Since Alex was obviously waiting for him to elaborate, Fred continued, 'Some people say all her real friends are long dead.' Alex looked on. 'Look, people like her...' Fred scratched his head contemplating his choice of words, not wishing to speak ill of the dead, 'People like her...well, they change their friends as often as they change their faces, if you know what I mean.'

'Um,' Alex thought he knew well enough 'but what exactly do you mean about all her friends being dead?'

'She always denied it,' Fred went on 'that she had known them of course. Said they were just confused cos she looked just like her mother or her gran or whoever,' he slowly shook his head, 'Wasn't true. My old great grandfather knew her.'

Alex was glad he had called in sick. He couldn't face work. He needed to sort things out with Mia. Make things the way they were before. He had called his in-laws first thing. Herb had told him gently to give his wife some space. That she had been through a lot. That now was not the time to be racing in hot pursuit. Swallowing his male pride Alex had deferred to his father-in-law's wisdom and even managed a thank you for the advice.

In any event Mia had just called to say that she was coming over. He sat surfing the net. He was going to find another of those witch balls. He knew that Mia had liked the shiny orb but had still been surprised by her reaction to its shattering. The kitchen was devoid of the broken evidence now. He was deeply engrossed in his online search of auction houses and antique shops. There didn't seem to be too many of these balls available. Still they were very old and rare. He wondered how many had met the same fate as the one that had previously taken pride of place in their patio windows had. He was ashamed of his drunken and juvenile act of destruction.

He found one. It was green. *How much?!* His action was going to hit his pocket hard too. He continued looking. A green one would not cut the mustard. There was a gold one. It was not round. It was egg shaped. No good. He knew that to even try to make things right he needed the ball to be specifically silver and definitely round. He learned that they came in different sizes too. Here was a tinted bronze coloured one. *Too small. Not silver.*

Mia's appearance made him jump.

'Watching porn?' she said without irony.

'Mia I didn't hear you come in,' he got up to switch the kettle on, 'No I thought I would try to find you a replacement witch ball,' he watched as Mia peered at the still open screen 'No point in hiding it. I had wanted to surprise you but no point in getting you all suspicious.'

The kettle steamed and flicked. He poured the coffee and took the two cups across to the table where she was sitting.

'Any luck?' asked Mia.

'Am still looking. Biscuit?'

She shook her head.

'It was stupid of me to smash it.'

Saying nothing she took a sip of the hot coffee.

'Look I will get you another. They are quite rare, I know that now but there's no point in being pissed with me about it. What's done is done.'

'Look I came to ask you for Jayne's address.'

'Jayne's address?'

'Oh cut the crap Alex.'

He sipped his coffee.

'Why?'

'I want to talk to her.'

'What about?'

'Look just tell me or I will find it some other way. Like you say no big deal.'

'You can't talk to her.'

'I can do what I bloody well like!'

'No Mia,' Alex paused to rephrase 'Of course you can do what you bloody well like,' he continued, 'but you can't do that....she's dead.'

Mia's blue eyes frowned.

'Dead? What do you mean dead?'

'Dead. The opposite of alive. Dead.'

'What happened?'

'She came off her bike. Impaled on a rusty old nail. Bleed to death on a fence,' he went on, 'She had no chance. Not many cars pass that way anyway.' Mia listened; so she was right he did know where she lived. 'She was concealed behind her car so no one could have seen her anyway.'

'How do you know this?'

'Fred told me.'

'When? When did this happen?'

'A few nights ago.'

'When?'

'I don't know. Think it must've been the night we came to the hospital.'

'The night I came around?'

'Probably I am not sure.'

'Look Alex when? This is important.'

'Why? Why is it important?' He didn't press the point he thought about when he had been in Fred's 'Yes I went to Fred's around the same time you came to in the hospital. Fred told me that they had found her.'

'Well how do you feel about that?'

'Bloody sad if you ask me. Nobody deserves that. She bled to death. Her shoes had turned red with her own blood.'

Mia saw the scene graphically in her mind's eye.

'Look I don't know what you expect me to say Mia,' he thought for a second, 'Nothing happened between us. She tried yes but you have to believe me,' he shook his head, 'nothing happened. I am not crying that she's gone. She was trouble. You tried telling me. She meant nothing to me.'

He thought he saw sadness and disbelief in Mia's dark shadowed, sleep deprived eyes. Jayne was the least of her worries but she was gone.

'About the witchball,' he went on 'I really am sorry.'

Mia wasn't angry about the witchball. She knew that his action in smashing it to smithereens had freed her. She had a fleeting thought to tell him which she dismissed. Pointless; he wouldn't understand. She knew that the key to her own freedom lay in those splintered shiny pieces he had cleared away. She knew without doubt now too that the pure evil contained within it, along with her, had also been set free again. Jayne was dead. She felt sure they were coming for her too now.

38

Perry's phone rang; it was Mia.

'Am I glad to hear from you.'

'Something is not right Perry. I really want to come down and see you.'

'No,' he interrupted her and it felt strangely odd saying no to her, 'you can't come here.' Mia listened, he never refused her. 'Look something is not right here Mia. You need to stay where you are.

'I need to get away. I need to think. I'm coming to see you.'

'You should be resting Mia. You need to be with your family. Be taken care of. I told you before, I can come to you.'

'Please Perry I just need to think.'

'What about the kids?'

'I told you. I can't be with the kids right now. It's not safe. Mum and Dad will watch them. I need to sort this out.'

'What does Alex say? Look Mia I really think you need to be with him and the kids.'

'Please Perry! You have to listen I am in danger! I can't keep them safe. I don't want them with me until I know that I can protect them.'

'It's ok I will come to you.'

'I need to talk to you. I was in the witchball Perry.' She just came right out with it.

'In the witchball?'

'It smashed. Jayne died. I came back. Whatever was in there with me, it was pure evil Perry I heard it…I felt it.'

'The ball smashed?'

'Alex smashed it. He threw my protection bottle at it and it smashed.'

'The piss bottle smashed?'

'Yes.'

'Mia. Do you mean they both smashed?'

'Yes the bottle broke and the witchball too.'

'Make another protection bottle. Do it now and keep it on you Mia.' Perry tried piecing the puzzle together as they spoke.

'Alex is getting me another ball. He feels bad. But he doesn't realize I wasn't in that hospital bed. I was in the witchball!' She cried between words. She was sobbing between gasping for air, almost hysterical now that she had said those words out loud, silently willing her friend to believe her.

'I believe you Mia. It'll be alright. I will come as soon as I can. There is something I need to do first.' He was looking at the photofit as he spoke but decided against telling Mia about the rape suspect which looked remarkably like Florence's nephew from the shop. She still didn't know that the old lady had died; now was not, he decided quickly, the time to tell her. 'Keep calm Mia. Don't tell anyone else they will cart you off to the nut bin. I will be there with you as soon as I can.'

Perry's heart was beating fast. That witch ball had history; a long history. He believed in the power that it held and that when it smashed, its evil contents would have been spewed back into this world. He searched in the bedside cabinet drawer finding the order of service from Florence's funeral. He scanned the back. There it was in small writing; the invitation to join the wake back at the house. Reading the address he knew the area. He would not shop the nephew to the police. He would go to him.

He felt sure now that what he had picked up that day was what he had suspected. Sick. Evil. Any demons held captured within that ball would at first be consumed with reaping revenge on she that had put them there; Florence. She had died and then her nephew had taken on their air of funk. He was sure that they had infiltrated his body, that they had been at the root of the change in his aura. That they had been responsible for the foul actions of this seemingly mild-mannered, overly judgmental granted but previously inoffensive man. It may be a pure coincidence that the e-fit looked the same but he had to know. He had to at least try to help the poor guy. For Florence. He would go straight on to Mia's from there.

Packing some clothes and looking through the bedroom window his eye caught his own gleaming witch ball. Opening the wardrobe he found a box of books and emptied them on the bed. Finding some bubble wrap in the bottom drawer he went downstairs to grab some brown tape and a pen and found the telephone number for a same day courier.

This couldn't wait.

Handing over the well packaged box to the driver he locked up and set off for Florence's house.

Where would she find a little bottle? She could go back to the house, make an excuse that she had forgotten something. See if she could find another little bottle or maybe something else suitable but that would only mean more questions. She had avoided asking how come the protection bottle was no longer hidden not wishing to place any importance on it. Alex was clearly holding back, he had not even broached the subject when their eyes had met across the table before settling on the now broken glass receptacle. No she couldn't face the questioning. Anyhow he was not stupid. She was sure that he would have at least suspected what it was for.

There were four charity shops in the High Street and it was in the third that she found the dusty little bottle nestled on the top shelf. She paid the fifty pence with a pound coin telling the assistant to keep the change. Three shops along she nipped into the hardware store where she grabbed a packet of nails and a small funnel. Her dad would have both but best not to risk having to explain, or worse, lie to him. She paid and headed back to her parents' place.

Perry pulled up outside what had been Florence's house. The exposed brick Victorian style detached property appeared quiet, the windows all closed and the curtains drawn. He wondered whether Peter was home. Standing at the front door he raised his hand towards the cast iron knocker. No modern doorbell. In keeping with the period the knocker was an imposing head of a green man, with ivy growing wild around the door and windows. For a second it was as if time stood still, his grasping hand just short of the knocker.

The letterbox started, slowly at first to vibrate, shaking then suddenly swinging fully as if penetrated by a forceful wind. Perry felt the invisible force in his solar plexus and in that moment it was too late.

He turned back towards his car with a new sense of urgency. All that mattered now was getting to Mia. He fired the engine and this now the only thought in his mind, set off to find her.

He usually stopped half way; to stretch his legs and have a bite to eat. Today the thought never entered his head. He had to get to Mia. And fast. He put his foot down.

Perry knocked on the door of Harley Sound. Alex answered.

'Perry. Nice to see you mate.'

Perry didn't have time for niceties. Pushing by Alex he was intent on finding Mia. He strode along the corridor towards the kitchen.

'What the fuck mate...' Alex's words were left hanging in the air as he closed the door and followed him. There was that rotten smell again.

Mia was standing with her back towards Perry as he entered. He said nothing. She instinctively felt the alien presence behind her. She had been opening the box that had just been delivered, peeling off the taped bubble wrap. Picking up Perry's witch ball from the box, it was smaller but just as shiny as the one that had fallen and smashed at Alex's hand. Holding it like a barrier, she slowly turned around. Looking Perry in the eyes she spoke slowly.

'Perry,' looking deep into his eyes she raised the witch ball, hands shaking fighting an invisible force field.

'Oh Mia!' Perry cried his voice suddenly mutating into a deep echoing wail, 'M..i..a' his voice now deeper and distorted.

Feeling like her head would explode Mia held the glass globe her hands shaking. The force was threatening to sweep it out of her hold. With all the will of her mind, as well as her hands she held it tight, hoping that it would not explode. She breathed deeply holding her gaze through watering eyes.

She watched as Perry's face, his beautiful kind and caring features, mutated into that of an old lady. Florence stood before her and smiled. She blinked as the vision blurred and melted immediately reformed into another and another. The contorted, twisted visions before her now she had seen before. In a dream? In a nightmare? No she knew them from within the witchball. She thought she saw Jayne's face and heard her familiar cackle. The scream that followed was not Perry's but a blood curdling cry of a hundred sorry souls. Mia could not move. Alex watched on wondering what was going on as Perry's body slumped to the floor.

'Mia!'

Mia was frozen to the spot still holding the ball. She heard the faint faraway cry of Alex calling her name. In a second she came too, blinking hard at the sight of Perry on the floor. Alex was standing over him now. Panicking and searching for his phone, eventually dialling 999 with his shaking uncontrollable digits.

Saying nothing Mia sat down. She was calm. She knew her friend was already gone. She watched without emotion as Alex called for an ambulance. She watched as he checked for a pulse, for any signs of breathing; for any signs of life. She stared into space. Soon in the distance she heard the wailing of an ambulance siren. Placing the witch ball carefully back in the box she covered it with the plastic protective packaging and resealed the lid. Then walking backwards, not taking her eyes off Perry lying there, still and dead, she gave up.

In all the commotion of the minutes that followed, the medics failed in their vain attempts to revive her friend, right there in front of her on the very arty black and white tiles that he had admired so much. His blood spilled neatly from the tiniest cut to his head. It struck her again how well the colour red went with black and white. He looked like a fallen chess piece on the outsized board that was her kitchen floor. And all the time she was staring ahead not blinking. Was she even breathing, herself? Pearl came through the door.

'Mia! What on earth has happened!' her question elicited no reaction from her daughter who failed even to appear to register her presence. Taking her by the shoulders she shook her calling her name once, twice; nothing. 'Mia' this time she shouted bringing her open hand sharp across her daughter's cheek, snivelling 'I'm sorry darling' before immediately resorting to, once again, shaking her daughter.

Having given up on the snappily dressed man on

the floor, the paramedics turned their attention to the now hysterical woman.

'Calm down love,' the taller one of the two spoke to Pearl, 'she's in shock'.

His mate, shorter and more rotund, nodded in agreement before suggesting, 'Put the kettle on love, think we could all do with a nice cup of tea.'

Alex watched on helplessly. She was his wife and yet in that moment he didn't recognize her. She looked smaller, almost like she was shrinking before his eyes and sat as still as if time had stopped. She was as pasty white as the white tiles save for an angry red hand print that materialized as it crept across her face.

'That's better now you let us get on, we see this type of thing all the time. White three sugars for me love. Don't suppose you have any custard creams.'

Alex shot a look to paramedic Hardy but stopped as his attention went to Laurel who was now frowning and shining a small torchlight into Mia's unblinking eyes.

Her sanity was the chink in her armor and Alex knew it. Here she was sitting on the edge; that much was clear to him. And yet, after all that had happened years before, something stopped him now from accepting the truth before him.

She stared back at him as she slowly rocked back and forth. Why wasn't he speaking? Now was the time to take action, shout, scream, call her mad, tell her she needed help! Instead he stood there prostrate; how it riled her. Why now, when those words and such action would be deemed appropriate did he just stand there like the cat had got his tongue?

He thought back to that time in Australia when she had walked away, finally acting on the threat he had doubted she would ever carry out. But she had. After the three month tug of war, she had let go; thrown in the towel with not so much as a foot stomp or a 'fuck you!'. It had taken twenty four hours, a whole day in flight but then that day had turned into weeks and then months. The days between them were upside down, ahead, behind, skew whiff and out of sync but she, free from her antipodean cage, breathed and blossomed once more. It was his cruel last low blow that had done it, calling her mad, a manic depressive. To question somebody's mental state is a tough call when justified; it is merely a cheap shot when it is not. His daring unharnessed nastiness had given her a gust of energy, and the gusto, to up and go. Already chomping at the bit, she ran; she didn't look back.

Looking at her now he saw that she was not there; he had lost her again, maybe this time for good?

39

Perry stared into the darkness. He felt light. Hearing distant cries and howls for a second he felt scared. He was not alone. What was happening? His fear subsided as quickly as it struck when beside him he felt a comforting warmth. Instinct told him that it was Florence.

Florence had felt Perry's honesty and faith immediately it had permeated the witchball. His smell was sweet amongst the foul foisty stink that had been all around her. She drew strength from the presence of his good energy. She smiled, her warmth expanding in the darkness with colours that Perry could see as moving golden vibrations as bright as the sun. Drawn towards it he felt its welcoming warmth and was immediately dissolved into it becoming at one with it.

Together they watched in wonder as a tiny glint of white light grew in intensity. At one now they were within its sights and held in its magnetic trajectory. It beckoned them. Ready for what came next, they both stopped struggling. Leaving the darkness and the screaming howling voices behind, together, they floated towards the white light.

40

Looking after the children was beginning to take its toll on Pearl. Herb helped as much as he could but they were not as young as they used to be. The school runs, Grace's nightmares and Ben's increasing curiosity, as he constantly explored 'why?' had fast become his favourite word. He asked after his mother often and Pearl felt unsure of how much information his little impressionable mind could take. Grace on the other hand hardly ever mentioned Mia at all.

Herb had insisted on visiting Mia alone in the hospital. Hospital. How times had changed in this new world of political correctness into which she had found herself thrust. A distant aunt had been in one of those hospitals years ago although they were never called hospitals in those days.

Pearl thought back to her own late mother's poor judgment at taking her there when she was only a little girl to visit dear old Aunt Rene. The memories had never left her. The strange men and women walking around heads hung low like zombies. Only now as an adult could she be at last thankful that she'd had the experience for it had taught her that these places, no matter how much they may have changed over the years, were no place for children. Even if it was their own mother in there.

She thought it one of life's most powerful lessons that the significance of events sometimes took a lifetime to unfold. In this moment she saw with clarity that was why she had been subjected to that awful afternoon, years before. She would protect her grandchildren and they would never have to deal with such awful memories. She would not allow it. Alex had collected the children earlier and taken them out for the day. Her stomach gurgled with nerves reliving the childhood memory. Today she would have to face them head on when they visited Mia. She felt the sickness in the pit of her stomach begin its journey north as her mouth filled with water and she just about made it to the bathroom in time.

Herb and Pearl drove to the hospital in silence. The large imposing Victorian building came into view as they started up the long sweeping drive. Parking up, Herb pulled the handbrake and took his wife's hand. He noticed she was wearing the string of pearls he had given to her on their wedding day. He had watched, as over the years, her hair had turned the same oyster shade of the pearlescent beads.

'Now I want you to prepare yourself Pearl. She is not well but this is for the best.' He was trying his best to comfort his wife and assuage the guilt within himself that he had allowed his little girl to be put in such a place.

'She shouldn't be here. We should be looking after her.'

'These doctors, they are trained. It's for the best.'

Walking up the big stone steps they found themselves in the reception. Pearl heard their footsteps as the sound resonated on the stone floor, echoing up to the high ceilings in time to her thumping heart.

Mia sat in the soft room curled up in her favourite white corner. She had four to choose from. She couldn't think. She could hear her breathing. *The doctor had come in earlier or was that yesterday?* She remembered that they had given her an injection 'to relax her'. *Did they say that her parents were coming?* She thought that she had seen her father but wasn't certain if that was a dream. Surely he would have taken her home if he had been here. He wouldn't have left her here, not her dad. She heard the door open.

'Hello Mia. Your parents are here to see you. Remember?' said the nurse.

Mia said nothing as the orderly helped her to her feet.

'We are going to take you to meet them in the garden. You would like that wouldn't you Mia?'

Outside the door she saw the wheelchair. Her legs shaking and weak she didn't object as they guided her into it. She felt like a rag doll with the stuffing missing.

Pearl and Herb sat waiting in the landscaped garden. Pearl scanned the handful of other people and patients looking for that familiar far away look in their eyes. It was there, ever present, that glazed vacant look and it made her shudder. Turning she saw the familiar figure being wheeled towards them. Meeting her daughter's eyes she saw that they too held the same cold and dead expression.

'Hello Mia love.' Herb spoke first, bending down he embraced his daughter.

'Mia.' Pearl, kissing her daughter on the cheek, looked at the matted formerly golden curls that used to be her daughter's pride and joy. She reached inside her bag grabbing a tissue to wipe her weeping eyes before Mia could see. She needn't have worried. Mia merely stared ahead as Herb held her hand.

Digging deeper in to her bag Pearl was searching for a comb. Panic started to rise. She needed a comb. She needed to brush her daughter's hair. Her shaking, probing hand finally locating the familiar shape, she took out the comb. She stood behind Mia and started to untangle the curls as she had done when her daughter was small. Only this time her daughter didn't flinch and cry out as she combed out the tangles. Saying nothing Herb watched as his wife's tears silently flowed. He was shocked to see that his daughter's auburn red curls now matched his wife's and those pearls.

Trying to take his mind off the events of the day Herb started to download some photos. He needed the space, his memory stick was full. He grabbed his little notebook. Mia had made him some notes, when she had been well, just some little prompts to help him. 'Step by steps' she had called them. He traced the curve of her handwriting with his finger. She had reassured him that she too needed to look stuff up herself, that unless you do something often enough until it becomes second nature, that it was easy to forget. He grew frustrated and gave up, almost launching the laptop and camera, on several occasions. This time, though, it was easy, he didn't even have to read all of Mia's prompts. His mind occupied, he found he was laughing at himself, easy when you know how, hey. He started to save the images to the laptop and flicked through the shots, printing the good ones out as he went.

He came to some that he had taken at Mia's house. The ones of the chandelier; the one with the light on had come out well. Very arty he gave himself another imaginary pat on the back. The close up of the glass droplet was a rainbow of colours and twinkles. He printed off a couple of those. Then he came to the ones of the large silver ball. Flicking through he saw the reflection of Ben on the floor, the background outline of the kitchen. *Very artistic, very arty farty.* He was getting good at this.

Clicking on the next one he did a double take. Looking closer at it he thought he saw Mia's face. He hit the print button. *Must be a double exposure.* Picking up the print he looked at it closely. Yes her face was there, clear if slightly smudged, peering down from the silver ball. *Um.* He thought digital was foolproof. *No double exposures my eye.* He scratched his head. *Could digital cameras take a double exposure?*

41

She slavered the cold cream across her cheeks. Her skin moved with the wibble wobble texture of a custard tart. She peered into the little hand held mirror. She had come across it again recently remembering that she had bought it in Thailand on one of her carefree trips many, many moons ago. Last time she had looked into it her skin had been plump and defined. For a second she thought she saw her younger self, an imprint projecting from the mirror waiting patiently for her to unsnap the catch. But it was just her imagination; she looked old. Cracking a forced smile she watched the lines crinkling in a crease like a raised blind. Letting her false smile drop she repeated the action three or four times as she studied her crepey, almost paper thin skin.

Her mother had always told her that losing too much weight was aging. Too much worry had turned her emaciated and stick thin. After years of carefully watching her weight she now wondered if there wasn't some benefit to those that went the other way and comfort ate.

The room was dark and dusty. Cleaning seemed, more than ever, to her a waste of time. Dust and dust still comes. Like anything in life a constant roundabout of doing the same things over and over. She couldn't see the point when she was younger; now was no different. Cobwebs clung to the ceiling and across the wooden slated blinds which hadn't been raised for years now. She wanted to keep the outside world out. Inside she felt safe. She heard the sound of a black bird shrieking outside. She thought the wild cats must be playing games with them again. She hoped that they would fly away for they risked being her latest present. She lit the two white candles on her alter.

She felt like her relax switch had broken; jammed at some 80 degrees on the scale of scared to manic. Her primitive fight or flight instinct had failed to get her out of danger - there was simply nowhere to run to and the unwinable fight had left her adrenaline fatigued and exhausted.

She saw jumping beans of blackness everywhere. These dark energy sparks that still occasionally fused when they came into the orbit of others, massing and mutating into evil before her eyes; she couldn't watch. On occasion she had found herself wishing for blindness; anything to stop the visions which were everywhere and non-escapable.

She took to staying in the house as much as possible only venturing out to her garden after she knew that Clive the postman had been. She had learned his name when he had introduced himself when he had to deliver another ball to add to her collection, too big for the letterbox. He was chatty;

open and friendly. She had stood half concealed behind her front door almost chomping at the bit to close it again.

'Clive I'm pleased to meet you...ooh I don't like that,' he had spotted her gargoyle on the shelf, fangs exposed, eyes wide and forked tongue extended, 'Very scary.'

'That's the point,' she spoke in flat tones her voice, to her, sounding amplified for this was the first time she had spoken aloud in weeks.

'I know, I know,' the postman continued his eyes glued to the stone statue, his mind buzzing with stories of this strange old woman. Perhaps the rumours that she could cast a spell on you were true after all; although in the flesh she didn't look that old. 'I know they are supposed to ward off evil spirits. Bye then.' He was up the path and away before she even had time to close the door after him; funny she never saw Clive again after that day and her postman never seemed to be the same person.

The hospital had wanted her to continue treatment as an outpatient. Although the heady cocktail of drugs brought a well needed respite from all the madness, to continue living in such a sedated way was tantamount to a living death. Zombied and standing statue still, her life had stopped; she longed for the music to start playing again. Looking around at the witch balls she thought of Perry and Florence, glad that they at least had each other in there. She could do nothing except keep them safe forever...

EPILOGUE

Abandoning the steaming shepherd's pie, Paul pulled on his kit and slid down the pole; even after all the years at the station he still enjoyed that. The adrenalin kicked in as the engine's siren wailed out their familiar warning.

He knew their destination. The funny old house on the hill; the one they said was occupied by an old witch.

Mia had woken to the crackle of fire and smoke. Scrambling down the stairs she stood, frozen in fear, eyes wide. The living room was a glow of licking orange and red flames.

There was a clear path to the door so, holding her hand over her mouth, she made a run for it.

Pop. Pop. She looked up as she ran. Pop.

With eyes wide in horror, through the dancing smoke, she saw the row of witch balls popping and melting in the blistering heat...

THE END

ABOUT THE AUTHOR

At the time of writing The Witchball her debut novel,
Frogmella Divine lives in Brentwood, UK.

Life threw her a curved ball. She took it.

She is currently adapting The Witchball into a
screenplay and contemplating the sequel.

Made in the USA
Charleston, SC
20 February 2014